THE MOST WONDROUS
LIGHTHOUSE
OF STRANGE DELIGHTS

Kingsley L. Dennis

Beautiful Traitor Books

The Caravan

1

The Oasis

The Caravan

2

ONE

Rodriguez's Dream

*L*uis Rodriguez Rodriguez had a dream, a vision, and it spoke to him so powerfully that when he awoke in the morning he had wet cheeks where his tears had been flowing in the middle of the night. There was something magical about the dream and it stayed in his mind and would not leave. It was as ridiculous as it was beautiful. And when you have a dream that lingers, you know only too well how difficult it is to let it go. A real dream lingers like a permanent fragrance in the air. And that morning Luis Rodriguez Rodriguez woke up with the most vivid scent he had ever smelled in his entire life. It reminded him of the scent of fresh herbs his wife used to plant in their garden. Luis Rodriguez Rodriguez had received a vision; and he was certainly someone in need of one.

The rest of the day he had sat on the back porch observing the springtime flutter of birds. The playful romance of winged creatures made him feel better despite it reminding him of the time when the love of his life was still alive. Yet since her passing, Luis Rodriguez Rodriguez had been a man of only half a heart, and with a longing so deep it made his boots feel heavy. The other half of his heart, the part that still beat within his chest, belonged to his beloved daughter, Rocio Rodriguez Rodriguez. It wasn't always the case that partners who married already happened to share the same surname. But with the two Rodriguezes it was an unfortunate but amusing coincidence. Yet, they had reasoned, what better sign did they need to show that they were destined to be together? Rodriguez Rodriguez was just fine. In fact, it was better than fine. And Rocio Rodriguez Rodriguez was even finer.

Luis Rodriguez Rodriguez waited for his daughter to return home, so he could share his dream with her. More than that, he wanted to tell her what he had decided to do about it. No more easy hours sitting on the porch observing the world pass by. No more idle immersion in the myriad of shapes, sizes, colors, and smells that formed the bubble of his days. Something had awoken inside Luis Rodriguez Rodriguez and it was calling out to him to engage once again with the world. This sparkle inside wished for him to be his daughter's wayfarer. To be her minstrel, her troubadour and warrior of light for all those missing a little illumination in their lives. For the first time in a long time Luis Rodriguez Rodriguez felt an excitement within. It was as if his river of dreams which had dried up to a trickle after the death of his wife was now beginning to flow again. The trickle had grown into a small stream and it was washing away the silt from his insides, making him feel fresher and more alive.

Luis Rodriguez Rodriguez smiled to himself; then he chuckled; and finally, he broke out into a huge laugh that echoed out into the vegetable garden, among the newly planted onions and between the baby spinach leafs. Finally, his broad laugh came bouncing back and washed over him, engulfing him in newfound joy. Luis Rodriguez Rodriguez jumped out of his chair and leapt around the garden like a child again. It was beautiful – it was all so beautiful. More than that, it seemed so *right*. And it made so much sense.

'Papa, that makes no sense at all.' His daughter Rocio looked up at him. Her deep dark eyes squinted in her oval face. She looked at her father, trying to fathom some meaning.

'I know it sounds, well, a little odd,' said her father.

'Odd? It's more than odd…it's downright crazy, Papa.' Rocio did her best to keep a calm voice so as not to upset her father. She knew he needed a dream, something to keep his spirit alive; something to make him feel a living part of the world. But this?

'But isn't it beautiful?' Her father let out another chuckle like he couldn't help it. It had just risen in his throat and like the best of escape artists it had pushed through his mouth and through the thin space between his lips. His eyes twinkled; two brown polished orbs glistening. It was as if they were trying their very best to sparkle-influence Rocio into believing in his plans.   Rocio regained her composure. Was her father going mad? She had never seen him like this before. It was good that he was so animated, so alive, but it was like he had swallowed some brain-fuzzy pill that made him all giddy.

'I'll make us some dinner, Papa, and then you just relax.' Rocio walked into the kitchen and began to prepare a light evening meal. It was not every thirty-three-year-old girl who lived at home, yet Rocio had chosen to move back to keep an eye on her father. She had placed her deft cooking skills to good use keeping her father fully fed and, considering all things, reasonably happy. A house is just not a home without a woman's presence, reasoned Rocio. And in that, like many things, she was right. For Rocio had a keen mind, a small frame, but a big, wide-open heart that could catch the tiniest of lost, stray particles as they floated past. Rocio was always caring for the lost, whether they were lost frogs, caterpillars, or the small salamanders that crawled into the house to hide behind the picture frames. Maybe they didn't want to be found, preferring instead to hide unnoticed in the shadows. But ever since she was a young girl Rocio had made a point of finding these 'lost' salamanders and bringing them back

6

to the light of day. Rocio had many friends in the garden of her youth; of all shapes, sizes, colors and shades. That night she made a special dish of soft potatoes lightly marinated in lemon with a dash of basil; a dish she knew her father loved. And that night she blew extra love into the potatoes in the hope that the breath of her heart would help to unwind the spell of craziness in her father's mind.

The next morning Rocio found her father busying himself in his study, a pile of papers lying on his untidy desk. By the look of him she guessed he had been up either most of the night or since very early in the morning. Such behaviour was most unusual. He must really be taking his dream seriously, thought Rocio. And that may not necessarily be a good thing - or anything.

Rocio brought in the toast drenched in olive oil, sure to get her father's fingers all greasy. It was a Saturday morning, so oily fingers were acceptable.

'Ah, Rocio, a beautiful new day!' exclaimed her father as he bounced over to her. 'I've been working on the first design. I thought it best to start from the bottom up, instead of the top.'
'Always a good idea to start at the beginning,' said Rocio with a wise warning look that only observant women can make.

'Yes, yes, sure – of course. Start where we mean to go on. Start solid and then build tall.'

'And how tall do you plan for this lighthouse of yours to be?' Rocio thought it best to seem to be going along with the plan. Any disruption now may only bring back her father's heavy air of despondency that had been hovering over him for far too long.

Her father paused. The mind of Luis Rodriguez Rodriguez was churning over data the way only an architect's mind can. You see, the mind of an architect is different from other minds. Some minds think in squares, others in straight lines. There are even those minds that think in curvy bends that can go around corners. Yet an architect's mind thinks in three spatial dimensions with mathematical numerals flashing through – just like birds fluttering between trees. The next thing an architect's mind has to ask is: can it work? They rarely, however, get to the question of: how much will it cost? Cost, you see, is a thing for other minds; the type of minds that think in zeros and ones, with a few dots thrown in for good measure.

'Sixty-two feet,' said her father eventually. 'Besides, it's not the height that really counts. It's how bright it is. The secret is in the illumination, not in the bricks.'

'Sure, Papa, but why sixty-two feet?'

A faint smile appeared on her father's face. If it wasn't for his moustache Luis Rodriguez Rodriguez's face would have looked child-like. The hair he proudly wore above his top lip was a guard against his boyish charm. 'It is the number of years your dear mother illuminated her own light upon this world.'

Rocio sighed. She missed her mother desperately; more than all the winged creatures in the world…more than all the four-legged friends, two-legged lovers, and more than every sweet word her father used to whisper to her as a child. But that was life, however you looked at it. And Rocio knew that life had its own task ready in wait for her. As soon as she had sorted her father out.

'Papa, I'm neither an architect nor an octogenarian; so, tell me properly how high sixty-two feet is.'

Luis Rodriguez Rodriguez sighed. 'Ah, the youth. Well, it's about nineteen meters, more or less.

'Thanks, Papa.' Rocio left the room leaving her father to get on with the inevitable job of greasy-fingering his new drawing papers. She went outside to clear her mind a little. Standing under the rays of sunshine she looked for the neighbor's cat that always tended to wander in around this time. Sure enough, Neko the cat could be seen sauntering amidst the pines, on the lookout for inobservant mice. Good, thought Rocio, at least something is still normal around here.

Luis Rodriguez Rodriguez was not to be dissuaded. He was now a man inflamed with a dream so vivid that he could still feel it burning iridescent behind his eyes. All weekend he had worked with animated energy, producing sketch after sketch of how his lighthouse would look. This was much to the agitation of Rocio who took care of everything else.

When Sunday evening arrived Luis Rodriguez Rodriguez found his daughter sitting on the back porch reading a book. 'I think I've got it,' he said, pushing a handful of papers into her lap.

Rocio looked at the grease finger-marked papers. 'Got what?'

'The lighthouse, of course! It's going to be the most wondrous lighthouse the world has ever seen.' Her father beamed at her as if he were the King of Persia.

'Yes, Papa, a lighthouse is all good and fine. But why in the desert? Why did your dream tell you to build a lighthouse in the desert?'

'I know, I know how crazy it may sound. Even I didn't believe the dream at first…but then, well, it's brilliant! Don't you see - it's the perfect place? It has to be there.' Luis Rodriguez Rodriguez clapped his hands together as if he were expecting a white dove to fly out of them.

'But Papa, nobody puts a lighthouse in the desert. There's no need for one there. You put them in or near the water to show people where the rocks are. That's what a lighthouse is for.'

Luis Rodriguez Rodriguez shook his head and bent down closer to his daughter. 'No, my dear, it isn't like that. A lighthouse in the water is for the visible things of this world.

It is to show people what is already there. But a lighthouse in the desert is a different story. It is to help people see what is not usually visible in their lives. To show people not what they ordinarily see but what they ordinarily *don't see*. That's what a true light is for. This lighthouse is for the human heart – it is not for the eyes.'

Rocio felt something stir within her; something she had not felt for a long time, not since her mother had passed away. She felt that sense of meaning, of purpose, that makes you know that not only is something worth doing but that it can be done, no matter how crazy it may seem. And now she began to understand just a little of what her father was feeling. It was the giddy pill she had just swallowed, and it felt…very, very good.

Rocio looked into her father's eyes and saw a twinkle that almost brought a tear to her own.

Luis Rodriguez Rodriguez came closer and whispered in his daughter's ear, just like he used to do when she was just a baby. 'We are not building something new. We are restoring something that is old…very, very old.'

Rocio looked up into the deep-set eyes of her father. 'Are you sure about this?'

Her father nodded his head and smiled.

'Okay, Papa,' said Rocio softly, 'let's make it happen.'

TWO

Across the Sierra

Rocio had everything packed and ready to go. She knew that when a decision had been made the next best thing was to act upon it. Delaying a decision only caused impatience. And impatience would give doubt a chance to creep in through the inevitable cracks. Luis Rodriguez Rodriguez was as happy as any man could be. He had spent the last few days in a flurry of sketches and calculations. He almost seemed to forget that Rocio was there at all, so occupied was he with his own tasks.

Rocio had given Neko the neighbor's cat a plate of fish leftovers as a way of saying *adios* for the time being. 'We'll be back,' she added, as Neko sniffed at the food. 'But don't expect us to be the same — people always change after long journeys. Take care, dear friend.' Neko meowed at the fishy delight and began to eat, licking her lips.

Her father peered around the patio door. 'All set?'

'Yes, Papa – just got to prepare some food for the journey.'

'Lovely! My favorite goat cheese it is then.' Her father went back inside and rummaged through his room a final time. Rocio raised her eyes to the heavens. 'I'm relying on you,' she said in a low voice. 'You said I could always count on you when I needed…well, I think we're going to need it now!' The sun shimmered, and a warm tingle rose up Rocio's spine and tickled the back of her head. Rocio had to smile.

The Rodriguez Rodriguez family line was well rooted in Andalusia. They had the Al-Andalus blood running through their veins. Perhaps this was why the idea of building a lighthouse in the desert was not so unusual after all, or so reasoned Rocio as they arrived at the beginning of the Sierra mountains. Over the Sierra lay the peninsula coast and the thin strip of water that separated them from the lands of northern Africa. The journey would be far enough, especially for a retired architect and his daughter. However, it could also have been further. Yet when all is said and done, a real journey is just as long as it needs to be. That's how to tell when a journey is genuine or not – it is neither too long nor too short. It sits in the Goldilocks range that is just palatable enough for the person, or persons, who dare to venture out upon its path. And a journey, like every fingerprint, is unique to each person. And the rest…well, the rest is taken one step at a time.

Luis Rodriguez Rodriguez stepped up to the rocky peak and stared out over the vast horizon. He pointed far out into the distance at the patches of white towns below.

'Look, Rocio!'

Rocio shielded her eyes with her hand and squinted. She too saw the swathes of land and scattered towns, like a hastily drawn map by a child's hand. 'What is it?'

'I can see our house from here!' Her father laughed giddily.

'Funny, Papa…' Rocio sighed. It was going to be an even longer journey if her father decided to add his unfunny jokes to it.

Walking the rocky ridge along the Sierra was pleasant as long as the sun shone down to warm the way. Both father and daughter carried nothing but a rucksack each upon their backs. Luis Rodriguez Rodriguez knew some of the mountain pathways as he had walked many of them as a child. His father, like his father's father before him, had taken their sons on many a walk through the mountains in an attempt to retain a connection with the Al-Andalus memory that soaked the soil. He was glad to be back again and breathed deeply to swallow the high mountain Andalusian air.

'Ah, there is nothing like her.'

'Like who, Papa?' Rocio was walking beside her father, lost in her own wandering thoughts.

Her father spread his arms out. 'This! These mountains are

our memories. They are the paths of our history. Like all the Rodriguezes we are carrying on family tradition.'

Rocio raised her eyes. 'Not this Rodriguez, Papa. You never brought me to the mountains.'

Her father suddenly stopped walking. A sudden shadow of sadness passed across his eyes. 'Yes, that's true. I'm sorry for that, Rocio.'

'I know you wanted a boy,' said Rocio calmly. 'It's okay Papa, most men do.'

Her father's mouth twitched. 'Aye…well, I did dream of a boy, perhaps. But love gave me a girl. And that was enough for me. I didn't need mountains to walk when I had a baby girl to love.'

'Yes, I know, Papa. You always were over-protective of me. But here we are now, walking the mountains together.' She smiled.

'Yes, here we are, at last. Now it's time to give these mountains some of our memories – father and daughter. Now's the right time, like never before!'

'When it happens, it's almost always the right time. That's why it happens.' Rocio playfully shook her head. 'Architects!' she said nudging her father as they continued walking. Sometimes she liked to tease the nerdy side of her father.

As they picnicked under the early afternoon sun they watched the vultures circle overhead. It was a clear blue sky and the birds glided through the mountain air streams. High in the Sierra everything seemed to know its place. Even the wandering goats stepped nimbly amongst the rocks with ease. They looked up and shook their bells before ignoring the two visitors. No doubt they were used to the appearance of human strangers upon their slopes. They didn't seem to mind – they had other matters to chew on.

Rocio liked the peace of the Sierra mountains. They were imposing and yet not oppressive. The mountains were stone philosophers, stoic and monumental. The world would carry on doing its thing, moaning and bemoaning, accumulating and wasting, producing and throwing away – and the mountains would just *be*. The rocks knew how to be patient. Persistence and patience were their great qualities.

As evening approached the two tired travelers came upon a small shepherd's stone cottage. Such cottages were not unusual in the mountains; they could be found scattered all around. They were the abodes of the Sierra folk, and often used by others passing through. Anyone could use them, for they could not be possessed. Inside they were simple and yet offered the bare necessities. Rocio and her father ate a little of the cured ham they had packed along with some bread. Their flasks still contained water and a little of the warm tea.

'Tomorrow we shall make a fire and boil some tea for breakfast,' said her father quietly. His eyes could just be seen through the darkening of the light. The cottage was intimate and cozy, and still warm from the day's sun.

'Papa?' Rocio's voice betrayed her tiredness. It had been a long first day.

'Yes?'

'You're sure you know what you're doing? With the lighthouse?' Rocio heard her father give out a low sigh. 'All I know is that I have to do this. If I do everything else in this world, yet do not do this one thing, then I will have done nothing. But if I do this one thing, then no matter what else I do in this lifetime I will have done everything.'

Rocio smiled. But her father could not see because the darkness had already fallen over them, soon followed by sleep.

The morning light woke them as it crept in through the small stone window. Rocio yawned first and stretched her arms. She could still feel the ache in her body from the day before. Her father soon followed with a louder yawn and a larger stretch. Then he raised himself up and clapped his hands together.

'A new day awaits us. Each new day is a blessed one.' Luis Rodriguez Rodriguez slapped his sides. 'Time to gather some firewood and make us a nice hot cup of tea,' he said as he opened the door and stepped outside. 'What the…?' He then quickly stepped back in again.

Rocio stood up and brushed herself down. Then she saw the surprise look on her father's face. 'What is it, Papa?'

Her father pointed. 'There's a man sleeping outside,' he said in a lowered voice.

Rocio shrugged. 'Well then, we better make enough tea for three.'

'Greetings! A bright blue day to you both.' The man took off his cap and scratched his bearded chin. 'Oh, and my name is Nash.' He bowed slightly, only a few centimeters, as if any more would over-strain him. The man appeared to be of middle-age, of medium height and build, and with a mischievous rugged face that looked as if it could lie to a thousand grandmothers.

'Nash?'

The man looked at Luis Rodriguez Rodriguez and grinned. 'It's a short form of a much longer name. But why waste letters when Nash is as good as any and better than most?'

'Why indeed.' Luis Rodriguez Rodriguez introduced himself and his daughter.

Nash bowed his head again, this time extending to one centimeter further. He then agreed to go out collecting a little firewood if the journeymen, as he referred to the two Rodriguezes, would share their marvelous urban tea, as he called it. Everyone agreed. Two donkeys brayed outside the cottage. Nash gave his best mischievous grin, then left.

'North Africa?' asked Nash as he sat by the fire with a warm metal mug of urban tea in his hands.

'Donkeys?' inquired Rocio as she supped on her tea.

The morning was still early, and the small fire served to take off the tiniest of chills that hung over the mountain slopes.

Nash shrugged. 'Taking them back to my family.'

'And where's your family?'

'North Africa.'

Rocio looked closer at Nash's appearance. Apart from being more rugged and weather-beaten, he looked as Andalusian as them. Nash noticed her close inspection.

'I have a large family,' he added. 'And you both – why North Africa?'

Rocio cast a sideways glance at her father, who stroked his chin.

'I guess you only have two options. You either tell the truth or tell a lie. Either is fine with me. I won't be judging you.'

Luis Rodriguez Rodriguez coughed nervously. 'Well, I guess we have nothing to hide, so I might as well say it as it is. We're going to build a lighthouse.'

Nash made a low whistle. 'Cool. And where on the North African coast do you plan to build this lighthouse of yours?'

When Luis Rodriguez Rodriguez didn't reply immediately Rocio spoke up.

'In the desert,' she said. And then there was silence.

Nash nodded slowly. 'It's one of those plans then, is it?'

'I'm afraid it is. It's the task I have to accomplish. If I do everything else but not this, then…'

Nash held up his hand to interrupt him. 'Sorry there, old fella. I know. I know what type of task it is. I had my task too…'

Nash's voice trailed off. Then suddenly he smiled. 'And I'm

going to help you on your way. I'll make sure I get the both of you across the water to the North African shores, or my name isn't Nashruddin al-Andalus!' Nash slapped his metal mug upon the floor. 'The deal is sealed – we travel together!' This time it was her father who cast a sideways glance to Rocio. Rocio smiled. 'Great – together it is then.'

The two donkeys brayed as they hobbled over the narrow rocky mountain paths. Nash led the way on foot as if he could walk the trails blindfolded.

'You've walked these paths before then?' called out Rocio from on top of one of the donkeys.

'Yeah, more times than the goats themselves,' called back Nash without turning around.

'Goats? Why the goats?' Luis Rodriguez Rodriguez was unceremoniously clinging on tightly to the neck brace of the second donkey. He looked less comfortable and more ill at ease than his daughter.

'These are all goat trails in these mountains. We walk where the goats walk. It's the goats that show the way.'

'And what if the goats become lost?' Luis Rodriguez Rodriguez didn't seem convinced.

'Then we get lost too,' replied Nash without hesitation.

Her father looked across at Rocio and frowned. Rocio

returned his look with a bright smile, as if to say I'm here because of you!

Despite his rugged ways and unlearned charm Nash showed a calm confidence and was attentive to his new guests. Rocio noticed, as only a woman can, that underneath his craggy exterior, Nash was a kind soul with a knowing heart. There was something about this simple donkey-shepherd, or whatever he was, that was contrary to the lazy human eye. And Rocio was nothing if not observant of such things. She had been watching her guide carefully, as she rode close behind on her new friend the donkey.

'Nash, may I ask you something?'

Nash lifted up his head but did not turn around. 'Sure, you may. Ask away, but answers may not be forthcoming.'

'That's okay, I'll take my chance,' replied Rocio casually. 'Earlier you said that you had also had your task…what was it?'

For a while there was no answer. 'Well,' said Nash after a long pause, 'that may be a tricky one to tell. I can't say directly but I can tell you where it led me.'

'And where was that?'

'It led me to what I'm doing now. And that also means that it led me right here to be helping you. So, it can only be a good thing, right?'

Rocio shrugged. 'I guess so.'

'Things don't always go one, two, three. It's more like they go one, ninety-four, four thousand and eighty-two, and back to five. Things that are real have a habit of jumping around. Only make-believe stories go from one step to another directly.'

'That makes sense.'

'Sure does. And it makes more sense once you've experienced it. You can't taste something until you've put it into your mouth and eaten it.'

For a while neither of them said anything. Nash walked ahead in silence, with Rocio on her donkey a little way behind him. And behind Rocio was her father, Luis Rodriguez Rodriguez, quietly concentrating on not falling off his donkey.

'All I can say is that I gave up everything for my task,' said Nash after some time. 'It was the hardest thing I ever had to do.'

Rocio regarded Nash as he walked in front of her. He walked with an air of confidence...and something else. 'And was it worth it'?

'Oh yeah.'

'And what has it given you?'

'Freedom. Real freedom.'

And that was the last time Nash spoke about his past. For everything else was now in the present.

The day passed as well as could be expected, given that donkey's backs are somewhat hard and uncomfortable. The mountain passes too were often steep with loose rocks. There were times when the three of them walked together, to give the donkeys a rest, or so said Luis Rodriguez Rodriguez. The air was thinner over the high passes, yet the views were spectacular. At one of the highest points they could see the waters glistening in the distance, and further away the shadows of land.

Nash nodded. 'Aye, that over there in the distance is the coast of North Africa. You can feel her beckoning to us with her charm.'

'And that big rock sticking out?' Rocio pointed below to the Iberian coastline.

Nash chuckled. 'That's what they call the Rock of Monkeys.'

'Why would they call it something like that?'

Nash turned to look at Luis Rodriguez Rodriguez. 'Well, it sure isn't because it's full of zebras.'

Rocio laughed. 'Full of monkeys then?'

'Monkeys all the way down. They say many a country has tried to conquer it, but the monkeys always fight them off. They're fierce warriors. I wouldn't mess with them myself.'

'But it's a part of the peninsula, isn't it? Luis Rodriguez Rodriguez didn't sound so sure.

'It's attached by rock only. But the monkeys own it. Aye, there are some things in this world that man cannot take for himself. And the Rock of Monkeys is one of them. Know thy place, that's what the monkeys are telling us.'

'And do they ever leave?' asked Rocio, now that her interest was aroused.

'Nah, they know better than that. Why would they want to mingle with us humans anyway? Besides, they don't have a passport!' Nash laughed out loud.

Luis Rodriguez Rodriguez and Rocio did not laugh. Their faces had suddenly turned pale.

'Oh,' said Rocio softly.

'Ah…' muttered her father.

Nash looked at them both, and then laughed even louder.

'Don't you worry about your passports – I'm going to smuggle you both into North Africa!'

'What?!'

'How?'

Nash brushed his frazzled hair away from his forehead. 'Cause I'm a smuggler, and that's what I do. Come on, journeymen, we've got some smuggling to do!'

The two donkeys brayed even louder than normal.

THREE

Smuggler's Crossing

The coastal waters greeted them like an old friend. They repeatedly lapped against the shoreline and retreated.

'I can see now why they're called waves,' said Rocio as she dreamily looked out over the waters. 'They keep coming, going, and coming; like a hand beckoning to you to follow.'

Her father Luis Rodriguez Rodriguez scratched his chin. 'I never thought of it like that.'

'Follow me,' said Nash with a grin.

The morning was warm and sultry. Rocio noted there was also something salty about it. A light breeze blew over the water that smelled like…

'Exotic birds.'

Both Rocio and Nash looked at Luis Rodriguez Rodriguez.

'That's what it smells like to me – exotic birds,' repeated Luis Rodriguez Rodriguez, breathing deeply. 'Ah, and it smells good too. There's nothing like it.'

Nash turned to Rocio. 'Did he ever keep exotic birds?'

'No. But he did keep a chameleon for a while, until he could no longer find it.'

Nash shrugged.

They walked further along the rocky coastline until it opened out onto a beach. For the first time in several days Luis Rodriguez Rodriguez and his daughter Rocio saw the sight of other people. In the distance several people were visibly enjoying the early sun.

'I think you should close your eyes as we cross this beach.'

Rocio looked across and saw her father's serious expression. She sighed and shook her head.

'Papa, sometimes you can be so ancient. I've seen naked bodies before, you know. I've even gone to nudist beaches myself sometimes.'

The look on her father's face would linger long in her memory. Inside, Rocio was giggling like a little girl who had just beaten her father at ping-pong.

Nash coughed into his hand.

'Best we get going now. We need to be over on the other side. On the other side of that cliff is a small bay. Nobody goes there. That's why we're going.'

Nash took the rope of the two donkeys and walked on. Rocio followed, with her father behind in deep thought.

You would have thought that a rugged-looking man pulling two donkeys on a rope, followed by a father and his daughter and all three fully clothed crossing a nudist beach might have drawn some attention. But it didn't. No one seemed to care, which was a good thing. The naked bathers were interested in their bathing, and the three travelers were interested in getting to their next destination. And then there was the tingling of bells.

'Bells? Is that bells?' Luis Rodriguez Rodriguez stopped to listen.

'Yeah, it's coming from the grass up there.' Nash pointed to a stretch of wild grassland that followed the ridge of the beach. It was as if the grassland had grown out from the sandy dunes. Or perhaps the beach had grown out from the grass as the one led into the other. Sometimes there's little difference whichever way around you try to look at it.

'Cows, that's funny!' exclaimed Rocio, and laughed.

Sure enough, several cows were roaming the grasslands, chewing, and causing the bells around their necks to clang.

'Cows on a beach! Now that's something you don't see every day.'

Rocio looked at her father and smiled. 'Yes, Papa; and when was the last time you were on a beach?'

'Point taken.'

The three of them, and the two donkeys, strolled past where the bell-ringing cows were chewing the cud and carried on until the beach came to an end. In front of them was the beginning of a cliff path.

'We need to go up and over there,' said Nash with brisk wave of his hand.

'And the donkeys?' asked Luis Rodriguez Rodriguez. He gave an incredulous look as if he didn't believe the donkeys could make such a steep climb.

'Ah yes, the donkeys are coming too.' Nash sniffed, and gave Rocio a quick sneaky wink that her father didn't see.

The path was not well-worn but was visible enough, or at least it was to Nash. They scrambled up, donkeys and all, until they finally arrived at the top. The cliff plateau was strewn with dry, spiky bushes that had been weathered by sea wind and scorching sun. When Nash next turned around he saw that Rocio had donned a large floppy hat with a toggle that went around her neck to tighten it. And she was now wearing a pair of dark, and quite cool-looking, sunglasses. Next to her was her father scrubbing his face with cream.

'Sun protector, factor fifty,' he said as he rubbed the cream into his face.

Nash looked askew at his two donkeys. The donkeys looked back and said nothing, not even a single bray.

'We're going to the desert,' continued Luis Rodriguez Rodriguez. 'We have to be prepared.'

'Makes sense.' Nash nodded. This time it was Rocio who

lowered her sunglasses just enough to give him a sneaky look, which her father didn't see.

After walking for a short time Nash stopped and turned to his companions.

'We have to be careful now, there's barbed wire up ahead. It's rusty and old, but it still cuts into you.'

'Why would there be barbed wire up here?'

'This is a military zone,' replied Nash casually.

'Military zone!' Luis Rodriguez Rodriguez looked at Nash, and then at his daughter.

Nash shrugged. 'It's been a military zone for a long time. They've look-outs along the coast here. But you hardly ever see any military types wandering outside their compound, which is over there somewhere.' Nash pointed away from the cliff edge further inland.

'Why here?' asked Rocio.

'This is where all the smuggling takes place. People, goods, you name it. It all comes over from North Africa to here.'

'And you are proposing that we smuggle ourselves over to North Africa at the very spot where the military are looking out for smugglers?' A tinge of uncertainty had crept into Luis Rodriguez Rodriguez's voice.

Nash grinned. 'I know – ingenious isn't it!'

Rocio and her father looked down at the small, enclosed bay below. It certainly looked beautiful as the clear waters lapped over the soft crystals of sand. Slowly, and with care, the three of them, followed by two donkeys, made their way down the narrow rocky cliff path.

'It's so beautiful!' Rocio stepped over the soft sand as lightly as she could, as if not wishing to disturb the many layers beneath her.

'It is,' agreed Nash. 'And you needn't worry; many feet have stomped over these sands and still this small bay preserves itself.'

'And does this place have a name?'

'Smugglers call this place the military beach.' Nash scratched his nose. 'It just seemed appropriate.'

Luis Rodriguez Rodriguez sat down next to his backpack and wiped his sweating brow. 'I didn't think about this part of the task. I only thought about the building of the lighthouse.'

Nash tied the two donkeys to a large jutting rock. 'Trust in your task but tie your donkeys first.'

Rocio pulled a face. 'Eh?'

'It's something we smugglers take care to remember.'

Rocio raised her eyebrows. She thought that if Nash was a smuggler then she was a juggler, which she certainly was not. All this time she had not seen Nash with anything more than a water flask and a torn jacket. The only thing he could be smuggling was himself – or Rocio and her father.

Nash smiled politely. 'Whatever your dream, whatever your

goal – whatever you truly believe in – make sure you have done your preparation. A person cannot live on air alone any more than they can fly without wings. You have to be grounded in this world before you go seeking the other. There we are.' Nash pulled at the rope to make sure it was firmly tied around the rock. 'Now, let's prepare some food. We have some waiting to do.'

By late afternoon the sun had lost its most potent strength. The hot midday glare had subsided into an orangey hue that radiated warmth over the rocks. Both Rocio and her father had taken a post-lunch dose in the shelter of the cliff shadows. They were tired from the long morning trek.

Luis Rodriguez Rodriguez awoke first. Sitting nearby was Nash, chewing on some grass and looking pensive. 'Any problems?'

'Nah. No problems – just patience. The boat should be coming in any minute now.'

'But it's still light. Shouldn't we be waiting for darkness first?'

'Nope. Darkness is for those who have something guilty to hide. Only those with fear move around in the dark. Real invisibility comes from being visible. True secrets hide themselves by being right in front of you, while everyone else is looking for them in the dark.' Nash let out a low chuckle.

Rocio woke up. 'What is it?'

'Boat's coming in.' Nash stood up and walked toward the gentle lapping waves. He waved his arms as a boat came chugging into view around the bay rocks.

'Get your things and let's be moving quick,' shouted back Nash. 'And whatever you do, don't say his beard is white!'

'What?!' said Luis Rodriguez Rodriguez and Rocio together.

The wooden motor boat pulled away from the bay and out into the rippling waters, bobbing and spluttering. The boat was neither large nor small; just enough room for a few guests and two passive donkeys. A large figure stood at the helm, his face turned away from the guests and focused onto the watery path ahead. Nash tied the donkeys to the rigging and joined his two journeymen at the rear of the boat. The sun was slowly setting, and a shimmering fell across the waters. Luis Rodriguez Rodriguez and Rocio looked at each other and smiled. They both shared the same thought. They were on their way. In front of them lay a huge dream; and in-between was water and sand. And yet they had made their move, and the world around them had responded. They were content, for now.

The large figure at the boat's helm turned around and eyed his guests through his one good eye. Over the other he wore an eye-patch. Across his face a large bushy white beard nestled like overgrowth. Rocio certainly thought he had an ancient pirate's look about him. The man tried to grin through his yellow stained teeth.

'Seems friendly enough,' said Rocio to her father.

Luis Rodriguez Rodriguez looked nervously at his daughter but didn't say anything.

'Allow me to introduce you both to Rufo; 'Red' Rufo as he is known. He's the wiliest, sturdiest, rogue-est captain this side of Monkey Rock.' Nash pointed over to the large man who gave a childlike wave. Rocio and her father both waved back.

'Red Rufo?' Luis Rodriguez Rodriguez gave Nash a questioning look.

Nash nodded. 'Yep, he had the reddest, bushiest beard you ever did see. It's his trademark – Red Rufo. There's no confusing him with anyone else.'

'And he's still Red Rufo?' asked Rocio in a whisper.

Nash nodded again. 'He doesn't know his beard is white. Good luck to anyone who should tell him.' Nash whistled through his teeth.

'But he's got at least one good eye,' said Luis Rodriguez Rodriguez, leaning over to join the conversation. 'Surely he can see that his beard is no longer red.'

'Normally, yes – but his one good eye is color-blind.' Nash smiled and then sat back and closed his eyes.

Red Rufo waved over to Rocio. Rocio waved back. Then he waved again. Then it dawned on Rocio that he wasn't waving *at* her, he was waving for her to come over. Red Rufo smiled broadly as Rocio approached. He pointed out into the waters not far from the boat.

'See that, girl?'

Rocio looked but didn't know what she was supposed to be looking at, or for.

'See there, where the waters meet? That there is where the Atlantic meets the Mediterranean. Look, see how the waters are different.' Red Rufo pointed again.

Rocio looked and this time she saw it. The two waters were of different colors. And it looked like they were separated by a watery line. On one side the water was darker, and on the other it was lighter.

'Wow!'

Red Rufo nodded. 'It's where sea meets ocean…but they don't mix.'

'Why's that?'

'One is denser than the other, so waters don't mix.'

'That's cool – never seen it before.'

'Water is like people,' continued Red Rufo in a halted, brusque voice. 'They're the same mix inside, but on the surface they don't mix. It seems odd, unnatural, but that's the way it is. Some of us are the ocean; others are the sea. We live side by side, but we don't mix.'

Rocio looked again at the line that clearly separated the same stretch of water into two parts, ocean and sea - two colors and a dividing line. Even the seas and the oceans are not impermeable to division, thought Rocio. It was both beautiful and yet oddly unsettling; like it shouldn't happen. But it did.

'Thanks, Red Rufo,' said Rocio, smiling.

The large man gave a nod and returned the most charming of smiles.

He may be blind in one eye and color-blind in the other, but he sure isn't blind, thought Rocio as she stood at the helm of the boat. She stared ahead into the watery dusk.

The lights were coming on over on the far shore. The sunlight had faded, and North Africa was beginning to twinkle here and there like scattered earthly stars.

'There she is – the beautiful land of North Africa.' Luis Rodriguez Rodriguez put his arm around his daughter's shoulders. 'Have I ever thanked you for coming on this journey with me? For helping to make this happen?'

'You just have, Papa. And what's a dream for if it cannot be shared?'

A little wetness crept into the corner of Luis Rodriguez Rodriguez's two good eyes. 'You're the bestest daughter anyone could have wished for.'

'Yes, but one's enough of me – don't wish for another' whispered Rocio into her father's shoulder.

A warm breeze blew to welcome their arrival upon the now not too distant shores. Red Rufo steered the motor boat into a small fishing harbor. Rows of young Moroccan men were sitting along the rocks sewing and mending their fishing nets. None of them looked up as Red Rufo moored and tied the boat. Only one or two heads raised slightly as Nash brought his two donkeys ashore. Everyone knew not to ask questions when a boat came in, especially when it was captained by Red Rufo. There is an unwritten camaraderie amongst such folk that is cemented by silence.

Luis Rodriguez Rodriguez turned to look directly at Red Rufo, the large, white bushy-bearded boat captain. 'I don't know how to thank you – or pay you,' he said, almost mumbling.

Red Rufo clasped Luis Rodriguez Rodriguez on the shoulder with his large hand. 'Nah, don't you worry about that. Nash tells me you have a task to complete – a once-in-a-lifetime-must-do-task. And that's good enough for me. One day we each are given our task. But not everyone listens. It's good you listen.'

Luis Rodriguez Rodriguez bowed his head appreciatively and began to move away.

'One thing.'

Luis Rodriguez Rodriguez looked back hesitantly at Red Rufo. 'Look after that girl of yours. She's a treasure.'

Red Rufo turned and walked away. Nash and his two donkeys stood at the end of the narrow wooden pier. A new land beckoned.

FOUR

Flamenco Caravan

The inn was already bustling with energy when they entered. Groups of people were talking nosily, each attempting to be heard over the rising clamor. Young waiters were dashing and weaving through the tables carrying metal trays with a variety of drinks. Yet the first impression that hit Rocio was the smell of sweat. She instinctively twitched and scrunched up her nose. Nash noticed the involuntary movement.

He laughed. 'That's the smell of anticipation...of desire, desperate hope, and longing.'

'You're sounding overly poetic,' replied Rocio with a note of sarcasm in her voice.

'There's nothing overly poetic when it comes to flamenco.' Nash's eyes lit up as he said that. 'Now grab this table here, and I'll be back.'

Rocio and her father put their backpacks down and sat at a round, wooden table. At first they felt uneasy, as strangers trespassing upon another's territory. Yet after a while they realized that no one was paying them any attention, least of all the waiters.

'I'm starting to feel anonymous.' Rocio gave her father a nervous smile.

Luis Rodriguez Rodriguez patted his daughter's hand. 'I think that's a good thing. Anyway, flamenco is from our land. We should feel at home here.'

'Home…?'

Rocio and her father sat in silence as the cacophony of the room seemed to increase with each passing minute.

Nash brought a chair over and sat down at their table. He wrung his hands together and smiled at his two traveling friends.

'Job done.'

'Job? What job?' Luis Rodriguez Rodriguez shook his head as if to ask the same question a second time.

'I've sold my wares…the smuggle is done. I'll be heading back out.'

Rocio laughed. 'You're a funny one, Nash. Why don't you just admit it and call yourself a traveler. You don't smuggle anything!'

Nash pretended to be offended. 'My dear child, I smuggle right before your eyes. Like I said, the best way to hide something is to make it completely visible, out in the open. When people are searching in the dark you can walk right past them. Walk right past them with two donkeys.' Nash grinned. 'Well, my path stops here. But you two must move on. I think there is someone you should meet.'

Nash stood up as a large, muscular, dark-haired man came over. The man nodded to Nash but didn't say anything.

'This is Diego. Diego Domingo. He's heading up inland and I thought maybe he could help you both on your way. I've told him a little of your situation.' Nash bowed. 'Señor Luis Rodriguez Rodriguez, Señorita Rocio – it has been my pleasure. May your onward path be illuminated. Oh, and when you finally get to an oasis full of donkeys, you'll remember me!'

As Nash walked away Diego sat down in his chair and eyed both Luis Rodriguez Rodriguez and Rocio with an air of suspicion.

'So, you're the man with the task, eh?'

Luis Rodriguez Rodriguez nodded. 'If I do everything else but not this, then…'

'I know all about tasks,' interrupted Diego with a brusque wave of his hand. 'But I don't take no fools with me.' Diego swiped a hand through his almost shoulder-length dark hair. Rocio looked at the man, at his greasy-looking hair and his steady, penetrating dark eyes. He could have been anywhere between forty to sixty years of age. His darkened face gave out no secrets, yet seemingly hid a storehouse of them.

'And we travel with no fools and no bandits neither,' said

Rocio as she leant forward in her chair. 'So, which are you?'
Diego was motionless for a moment. Then he laughed loudly.
'By my flamenco heart, you're a true bred Andalusian!' He
banged his fist on the table. 'We meet later, after the show
– if your hearts are still in your bodies.' Diego stood up and
strolled away with a confident swagger.

The heat and energy in the inn had risen to a high pitch of
sweat and anticipation. At its peak a young man appeared on
the makeshift stage. Carrying a guitar in hand he sat down on
the single chair. The whole room went quiet and all chattering
hushed. The young man's face looked intense. He hung his
head as if whispering low to his guitar some secret words of
love. Then he strung his fingers across the strings, picked and
plucked, as a melodic yearning called out. The guitar player's
face then tightened, his eyebrows twisted, and his fingers
unleashed a torrent of lugubrious longing.

The musical force was almost hypnotic, holding the
whole room enthralled and entranced. Rocio felt as if she
had forgotten to breathe, as she finally let out a long pent-up
breath. She looked across at her father and saw that he too
was motionless as if in a trance. And then she appeared.

The lady stepped out wearing what Rocio recognized as a
flamenco dress. She stomped her feet and the audience gasped.

Then what came out of her mouth slapped and stunned each face in the room. The lady looked similar age to the guitarist, and yet her dark hair ran down her shoulders in defiant curls and her voice was aged beyond her years. Rocio's own heart pounded in her chest. She had heard flamenco many times as she grew up listening to her father's music…but never like this. Rocio had always found flamenco melancholic and saddening. But here, in this live atmosphere, the energy was like a dose of passionate poison made sweet.

The guitar and the voice together submerged the listeners in a shower of emotional energy. And when the show was over the sweat had also been shared, for everyone's brow wore the telltale wet beads. Then the clapping engulfed the room in an immense wave.

Luis Rodriguez Rodriguez wiped his brow. 'That was intense. Magnificent. Worthy of the best.'

Rocio nodded. 'Yes, intense.' She let out another deep breath. It took some time for the room to settle down. Finally, a waiter came over and put down two glasses of what looked to be dark tea.

Luis Rodriguez Rodriguez looked up at the waiter. 'What's this?'

'Diego.' The waiter shrugged and walked away.

Rocio tasted it. It was sweetened tea with mint leaves. It was a welcome drink.

Moments later, the guitarist and the singer entered the room. They made their way through the tables and chairs to the far corner. They sat down at a table with Diego. They spoke a little together then looked over to where Rocio and her father were sitting. Diego motioned for them to come over. They collected their backpacks and likewise pushed themselves through the tight spaces between the tables. Diego pulled up two extra chairs and introduced his guests. The young guitarist was called Paco and the young singer was Lola. They were introduced as man and wife.

'You liked the show?' asked Paco in a surprisingly soft voice.

'Fantastic!' exclaimed Luis Rodriguez Rodriguez.

Paco nodded but didn't say anything. Lola eyed up Rocio.

'She sings?'

Rocio shook her head.

'Good. Only one singer here.' Lola lifted up a small thin glass and poured the contents down her throat. 'Task, eh?'

Rocio nodded and looked over at her father.

'Mm, I see. And you? What's your thing?'

'I play the harmonica,' replied Luis Rodriguez Rodriguez.

Lola nodded for him to continue. Luis Rodriguez Rodriguez reached into his backpack and pulled out his harmonica. He then looked around nervously as if afraid to disturb the others in the room.

'Play!' demanded Lola.

Luis Rodriguez Rodriguez breathed deeply and played a flamenco-sounding tune. Everyone listened. Paco clapped his palms together, and Rocio looked on surprised. She hadn't seen her father play for so many years. Diego scratched his cheek and nodded. When he had finished playing, only Lola spoke. 'You got soul – but stick to your task.'

A selection of plates arrived with different food. Everyone ate heartily.

'You can both share with Paco and Lola,' said Diego finally. 'You can travel with us for part of the way, and then you continue on alone.'

'Thank y…'

'No need to thank,' interrupted Diego. 'The task also runs through our blood, through our line. We understand what it means. We help those with a task on their way. So it has always been, so it will always be.' Diego nodded and stood up to leave.

Lola put her arm around Rocio's shoulders. 'Hey dear, let your Lola take care of you.' She then gave Rocio a big hug. Rocio thought she smelled like a mixture of jasmine, wild roses, and sweat. But she felt secure.

The early morning sun shone through a sharp blue sky. It was as if in North Africa the colors were intensified and rawer.

Luis Rodriguez Rodriguez and Rocio washed at the inn and ate a good breakfast with their new comrades, the flamenco troupe. Paco and Lola were more lighthearted and fun when not performing, yet it was obvious who had the control of things. Paco was more mild-mannered and a quieter figure than his wife Lola. And they both knew it. Diego Domingo was Lola's uncle, and also their somewhat business manager. Between them they had two decent-sized caravans, four horses, two guitars, and one incredible voice. And the rest was a life on the road.

'We travel by day, perform by evening, and dream the world into being by night,' said Diego as they were strapping the horses to the caravans.

'And you've always been on the road, like this?' asked Rocio.

'No dear, not always. Only when the lady demands it,' replied Lola.

'You mean…?'

'What she means,' continued Paco, 'is that the Lady of the Spirit demands that we spread her energy as best we can.'

'Aye, but not in every part. Just in the places that need her energy at that time. And right now, it's in these parts around here,' added Diego.

'And how do you know this? How is this knowledge given to you?' Luis Rodriguez Rodriguez's voice betrayed a certain amount of incredulity.

The flamenco three, as Rocio came to call them, all laughed.

'That's one of the secrets of our line,' said Diego.

Lola beat her chest. 'It's in here, dear. Everything you need to know is in here.'

And the caravan moved on.

Luis Rodriguez Rodriguez rode up front with Diego on his caravan, whilst Rocio sat with Lola as Paco steered the reigns of their horses. Lola and Paco were likely to be younger than Rocio, yet they displayed an aged presence, as if they were older souls. They behaved as if they were world-weary adults with a whole lifetime behind them. Perhaps, thought Rocio, they had already lived more than one lifetime in their young years. Lola sang as if she had known heartbreak and sorrow a thousand times over. And Paco played his guitar as if he had been burnt in the flames of the inferno below. All this made Rocio feel as if she had lived a sheltered life – a life programmed to be protected and secure. And here she was, following in the footsteps of her father's task. She was traveling into uncertainty with the unknown hope of polishing a dream.

Lola looked at Rocio as she sat thinking these thoughts. 'It's the task.'

'Eh?'

Lola nodded to herself and smiled. 'It's the task which is doing this to you. It affects people in this way. It affects more than just those given the task. It affects those people also who agree to realize it.' Lola pointed at Rocio. 'And that's you, dear.'

'You think so?' asked Rocio softly.

'Don't think so, dear – know so. Thinking is for those people who don't get involved in things. They stand at the edge while it happens, thinking about it. That could have been you, or your father, if you had just stayed at home thinking about your dream. But no, you both decided to do something about it. And that's what the task is all about...whatever it may be.'

Rocio thought about this for a while. Then she smiled to herself. She then told Lola and Paco about the task, to build a lighthouse in the desert.

Paco whistled a little tune when Rocio had finished. 'There's music in that dream.'

Lola agreed. 'There's something very right about it; something so right. If you think about it, then, well, it's all nonsense. But then again, a real task isn't about thinking it. But...but if you feel into it...well then, that's another thing! And then you know when something feels so right.' Lola slapped Rocio playfully on the shoulder. 'You, girl, got yourself a real task.'

'You mean my papa has got a real task.'

Lola laughed. 'My feeling is that the task is taking you along for the ride as well. Don't you feel it, sister?'

Rocio had to admit she did feel it.

Luis Rodriguez Rodriguez was enjoying riding up front with Diego and the horses. He enjoyed the smell of nature, as he called it.

'This is the real thing,' admitted Diego. 'Gasoline is more

expensive than horse feed, and stinks worse than horse manure. We prefer those things that live and decay like a real thing should. We don't put our faith in oily liquids or rusting metal. We live alongside those things that live, sleep, and die just like we do.'

'This too shall pass,' mumbled Luis Rodriguez Rodriguez under his breath.

'What was that?'

'Oh, just something I heard as a kid – this too shall pass.'

Diego looked over at Luis Rodriguez Rodriguez and studied closely the retired architect. 'That's something we say. It's one of our code phrases. How did you come across it?'

Luis Rodriguez Rodriguez shrugged. He couldn't remember when or how he had first heard of the phrase. He just had a feeling that someone had said it to him long ago. 'There's some real blood in you, son. Maybe that's why you're riding with us now. All things come around and meet up eventually.'

And the caravan moved on.

FIVE

Shepherd's Way

*I*t was a full day's travel inland, away from the coastal waters. Further away from the wetness and toward the drier terrain. The smell of the air slowly changed also as if signaling that a new land approached. The caravan passed many sellers with their stalls at the side of the dusty roads. Pottery and ceramics, large watermelons, and rock crystals were all hawked. The sellers, mainly young men, sat under makeshift sheeting to shield from the heat of the sun. The flamenco three would sometimes offer greetings as they passed. There was an etiquette of the road that was unspoken. This was an unknown world to Luis Rodriguez Rodriguez and his daughter. Yet they were under the protection and guidance of their caravan. Luis Rodriguez Rodriguez had a feeling that no one would interfere with Diego Domingo. There was something imposing about the man. He could instill uncertainty and confusion in a person; and fear too if he so wished. He could do it with just a look, a glance, or simply from his presence.

The caravan came to a halt as dusk was gathering up the last of the sunlight. The end of the day was near at hand, and yet the road ahead, like all roads, was timeless.

Diego lit a fire while Lola and Paco prepared the food. Not a word was spoken between the flamenco three as they put everything into place. It was as if they knew their roles and what needed to be done. There was no question of right or wrong; of wanting or not wanting. Things that needed to be done got done. Rocio and her father watched it all in silence. It seemed like a well-worn ritual.

Diego stoked the fire as Lola cooked over it. Paco brought seats for them all to sit around. They didn't need the heat of the fire for warmth, so they kept a reasonable distance away.

'The flickering flames are hypnotic.' Diego looked over at his guests. 'Flames such as these have kept humanity alive since the dawn of our time.'

'They have also burned us many times,' added Luis Rodriguez Rodriguez.

'That is true. One thing often brings the other; just as the love of flamenco brings forth its pain, its suffering. If one comes, so does the other…eventually.'

'But you can choose which one stays longer – the love or the suffering.'

Diego looked over at Rocio and smiled. 'You may be right there, sister. Love brings with it other treasures too.' Diego paused, looking into the fire. 'Let me tell you one of our stories; a story that we carry around in our blood. There's a lot in this story, as there is in all real stories. Stories are carriers of our true blood.' Diego cleared his throat.

'One day, an ordinary day like any other day, a woman stepped out of her caravan and saw three old men with long beards sitting at the side of the road.

'I don't know you,' she said, 'but you must be hungry. Please come into our caravan and eat something.'

They asked, 'Is your husband there?'

'No,' she said, 'he's out on an errand.'

'Then we cannot enter,' they said. Later in the afternoon when the woman returned she saw the same three old men sitting at the side of the road. She waited anxiously for her husband to arrive back and when he did she told him what had happened.

'Well, tell them I've now arrived back and invite them to come in. We have food enough to share for all. In these desperate times we can at least share a little of what we have. That is our way. So it has been and so it shall always be.' The woman went outside to invite the men to come in and join them.

'The three of us cannot enter together,' said the old men.

'Why?' asked the woman, wanting to know.

One of the men pointed toward one of his friends and explained, 'His name is Wealth.' He pointed toward the other and said, 'His name is Success, and my name is Love.' He then added, 'Now go inside and decide with your husband which one of us three you wish to invite to enter.'

The woman went back inside and told her husband what they had told her. The man, very happy, said, 'That's good! If that's the way it is, let's invite Wealth, and have him fill our caravan with wealth.' His wife did not agree. She said, 'My dear, why don't we invite Success?' Yet their young daughter had been listening to the conversation and from her place at the back of the caravan stepped forward with an idea. She said, 'Wouldn't it better to invite Love? Our home would be full of love then.'

'Let's pay attention to our daughter's advice,' said the woman to her husband. The husband immediately agreed for he loved his little daughter's gift of intuition.

'Good,' he said to his wife, 'now go outside and invite Love to be our guest.'

The wife went outside and asked the three old men, 'Which one of you is Love? Please come and be our guest.'

Love stood up and began to walk toward the caravan. The other two also rose and followed him. Surprised, the woman said to Wealth and Success, 'I only invited Love, why are you also coming?'

The old men responded together, 'If you had invited Wealth or Success, the other two would have remained outside, but since you invited Love, wherever he goes, we go with him. Wherever there is love, there is also wealth and success."

Diego poked the fire with his stick. 'Yes,' he whispered. 'If you truly follow your heart, the rest will arrive as well. That is our way; the way of flamenco is of the heart. Wealth and success is in the heart too, and not in your hand.'

A shadow from the flames flickered across Rocio's face just in time to hide the droplet in the corner of her eye. But Diego knew it was there.

The second day of the caravan found them moving on. Diego had said they were following the old shepherd's way. By late afternoon they should be at their destination. At the blue town.

'The blue town?' asked Luis Rodriguez Rodriguez as he rode alongside Diego.

'It's not very poetic of us, but we call a thing what it is. And this town is painted blue. So it's the blue town, and that's that.'

In the distance lay the scattered buildings that formed the town. The buildings clung to a mountain valley and, true to their name, were painted in hues of blue. As the late afternoon sun fell upon the town it looked as if it was going to disappear, only to reappear again in another location, on another mountainside somewhere. The town appeared so ephemeral that Rocio dared not take her eyes from it in case it should be gone when she next looked.

'Is this place real?'

Paco laughed and glanced over at Rocio. 'Is anything real?'

'That's not a very helpful reply.'

'He's got a point though, dear.' Lola smiled at Rocio. 'Things are as real as the stories that surround them. It's us that make things real. We told ourselves the world was flat once. Was that real? It's a fine line between the mystery and the real, and in-between there's every game with winners and losers. We make things real. Then we destroy them again.' Lola put her arm around Rocio, something that she liked to do often. 'Look at us. We make a certain reality every time we perform. Then we take it away again. Reality is being created and dismantled in every moment. And when it happens quickly enough, well… folks sense a type of permanence. That's reality. But is it really real…?'

Rocio frowned. 'I thought I'd asked a simple question.'

Lola slapped her thigh with her one free arm and threw her head back in sonorous laughter.

'Trust in fate, but tie your horses first,' said Diego as he tied up the horses from both caravans. 'Our path brings us here. This is where we'll be performing tonight. You two can make yourselves useful by feeding the horses.'

'I think we'll give your flamenco harmonica a miss this time.'

Lola gave Luis Rodriguez Rodriguez a cheery look whilst Rocio tried to hide her smile.

'And then maybe you'd both like to take a stroll with me through the town?' Rocio thought Paco's offer was a good idea.

The avenues were narrow and seemed to squeeze the cobbled streets into snake lines. The houses were built on top of each other as if they were all leaning in the direction of the person walking. The houses were painted in various hues of blue, some darker than others, and simple wooden doorways promised unknown interiors. Luis Rodriguez Rodriguez and Rocio walked almost in a trance as they followed Paco up and down stone steps, through archways, and past alcoves of sellers and small shops stuffed with local handicrafts. After a while it dawned on them that they had no sense of where they were, having left orientation long ago behind.

'Do you know where you're going, Paco?'

The young guitarist looked back at Luis Rodriguez Rodriguez and shrugged. 'Doesn't matter. All ways here eventually lead back. The secret is just to keep going. You'll only get lost if you start to return.'

'Seems like a good plan,' added Rocio.

Luis Rodriguez Rodriguez wasn't so sure, but neither was he inclined to argue the point.

Soon they passed a large archway that brought them out onto a path that perched at the top of the old town. All around them was a vista of mountains and possibilities.

Rocio let out a deep breath. 'Everything seems so open. When we were at home life seemed so closed in, so…so regular, so normal.'

Luis Rodriguez Rodriguez nodded. And for a few moments the two Rodriguezes shared a slice of silence.

'Sometimes you have to leave home before you can see the other possibilities,' said Luis Rodriguez Rodriguez to break the silence.

'Thank you, Papa…for this opportunity.'

'No, thank you. I needed you…to believe in me.'

'I'm beginning to think belief is overrated.'

Luis Rodriguez Rodriguez laughed. 'That's my girl!'

Paco was waiting patiently, leaning against an old wall, chewing on a twig. Rocio thought she recognized an agedness in him that hid behind his eyes. He was an older man really, just masquerading through this youth. At that moment a hooded figure appeared in front of Luis Rodriguez Rodriguez and Rocio and blocked their path. His hooded face was half concealed. The other half was dark-skinned and heavily wrinkled. His one visible eye looked all white, as if blind. He spoke in a cracked voice.

'Last night I heard a voice whispering in the darkness. It said there is no such thing as a voice whispering in the darkness!'

The hooded figure quickly hobbled away and disappeared through an archway.

'Let's go,' said Paco. 'We'll soon be performing.'

That evening another spell was cast. Magic was alive, and it weaved through the air that passed between Paco and Lola. Diego sat at a corner table intensely observing the performance. It was as if he was making sure that what needed to be done got done. For him, it was more than a flamenco performance.

'Food,' he said, turning around to Rocio and her father who were seated at the same table.

'You're hungry? You want to order some food?' asked Luis Rodriguez Rodriguez.

Diego shook his head and looked straight at the architect. 'No,' he said after a pause. 'This is food – the real type of food. This is what sustains people.'

Paco's guitar pierced through the crowded room accompanied by Lola's voice. Everything felt as if it were being scrambled. The stars were being rearranged and placed into new orbits. Star shrapnel was being flung off and was falling to the earth as fine dust. It was everywhere. It merged into streams, rivers, and mingled with the greatest seas and oceans. And, above all else, it was falling upon the Shepherd's Way. That evening a veil opened for the briefest of moments. Just long enough for something to make its way through. And then the gap closed again.

The people in the room erupted into rapturous applause. Paco and Lola left the stage looking exhausted.

Diego Domingo nodded his head in silence. He was content with the performance. Tomorrow they would be moving on.

It was an early rise. The sun had not been up long. As she yawned, Rocio thought she saw the sun yawning back at her. She looked into its glare directly for a few moments. Its light was not yet strong, and her eyes allowed its rays to penetrate without protest. Are you really that far away? she whispered.

'Some people say they can live on sunlight alone. Just water and sunlight.'

Diego's voice caused Rocio to suddenly snap out of her reverie. 'Still, I prefer to tie my horses first.' Diego continued strapping the horses to the harnesses of the two caravans.

After an early breakfast they started out on the road again. Luis Rodriguez Rodriguez was beginning to get used to riding up front alongside Diego. This is not a bad life, he thought. A person could get used to this. The freedom, the endless possibilities…the open road. Diego didn't say anything, yet he could observe the look on his companion's face. And sometimes a look is enough. You don't always need words to read a book. Some books are symbols resting against the shudder of thoughts.

The caravan moved on. Rocio sat beside Lola as Paco steered the horses along the roads that wove through the mountainous countryside. When they were high up the views were spectacular. Slopes of reddish earth curved like a creature's spine through the land. Lola was unusually quiet. Her usual animated mood was subdued. She would glance over at Rocio, sometimes giving a faint smile that while still warm was more distant than the day before.

'Where are we heading now?'
Diego looked at Luis Rodriguez Rodriguez. 'This is the third day of our caravan.'
'Ah, so it is. I wasn't counting.'
'No one's counting. It's just the way it is. And today we will part.'
'Oh, I see.' Luis Rodriguez Rodriguez fell silent. Then after a pause he added, 'quite right. You've already helped us enough. It's time to be moving on.'
'It's not like that. Three days with our flamenco caravan is all that can be given. Any longer and the balance is disturbed. You may not understand but everything needs to function correctly. And besides, any longer with us and you may lose

sight of your own fate. That can happen here. You must not forget why you came here in the first place.'

'Yes...of course – my task.'

Diego nodded as if he knew exactly.

'Yes, you're right. We must be moving on. I have a task to complete. Thank you for the reminder, Diego.'

'No thanks necessary. It's the way it is...and it's our way.'

The caravan halted for lunch at a fork in the road. The group of five people prepared the food without sharing any words. When there is little that can be said, it is often best to let silence say more. The feeling was not one of discomfort. On the contrary, everyone sensed a familiarity between them. Finally, after eating, Diego allowed a few words to slip out.

'We are now at the forking path.' He pointed to the split road at the side of which their caravans were parked. 'This is known as the forking path on the Shepherd's Way. It is so named because it is what it is. Here the path forks and each one takes the traveler to a different destination. It is also a place where people part to continue their journeys. Each path knows where the traveler wishes to go even before the traveler knows. What takes a person down their path is the decisions they make. Decisions make paths and paths make destinies, or destinations, depending on how far one goes.' Diego stood up and began to pack away their belongings.

Paco went to the back of his caravan and unloaded two backpacks.

Lola came over to Rocio and gave her a big, sisterly hug. 'On your way now, dear. You mustn't keep your fate waiting. She can be an impatient madam at times!'

'Yeah, I can feel it,' was all Rocio said. She didn't say another word as she gave Paco and Diego a hug and lifted up her backpack.

Luis Rodriguez Rodriguez thanked each of the flamenco three for their hospitality and friendship. Then he too took up his backpack and chose the forking path. The reddened earth of the mountain ridges beckoned the travelers onward.

Behind them the caravan moved on.

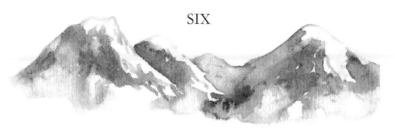

SIX

Keeper of the Fig Tree

Father and daughter walked along together, each in their own thoughts. What each had in their mind could not be translated for the other. Words were penniless. Luis Rodriguez Rodriguez put his hand upon his daughter's shoulder and smiled. He didn't know if he was smiling just to himself. He only knew that his daughter Rocio was the most amazing being in his world. Everything else was black and white.

Rocio was entranced by the colors of the landscape. If nature had been invented it would have been so dull, she reasoned. Only the real things could be so colorful, so alive, so unexpected. Like her father and his sudden dream and his vision for the lighthouse. That too had arrived unexpected. It seems that just when you least expect it, the universe springs a surprise.

Rocio adjusted the hat to shield her head from the constant touch of the sun. Luis Rodriguez Rodriguez had a blue scarf wrapped around his head that almost made him look like a seasoned explorer. Almost but not quite; and that was the difference. Odd, thought Rocio; her father hadn't had that scarf before. Perhaps he picked it up from the blue town. That that would make *some* sense.

'Is that a hawk?' Luis Rodriguez Rodriguez pointed up to a winged creature hovering in a wind thermal. 'Look. It's using the wind current to spiral higher.'

Rocio shielded her eyes and looked up. 'I suspect it's looking for prey.'

'Yes, conserving energy using a wind current while it searches. Amazing. Perhaps our lighthouse will be as high as that, with its searchlight spiraling into the sky.'

Rocio laughed. 'But Papa, not giving light to help search for prey I hope.'

'No…no, of course not. It'll be a light of wonder. A most wondrous lighthouse!' Luis Rodriguez Rodriguez slapped his hands together as his scarf slipped from his head and over his eyes. 'Ah, can't see…' he mumbled as he fumbled with the scarf.

Rocio stopped walking and her father almost ran into the back of her. She covered her eyes again but this time she wasn't looking high into the sky. She was staring straight ahead at a patch of fertile grass that stood out from the arid surroundings. And in the center of this lush, fertile patch stood a large tree which, somehow, looked familiar.

'Mm. Unusual, but nice.'

Rocio thought her father could sometimes be a bit sparing in his emotions.

As they approached the tree Rocio realized why it looked so familiar. They had the same tree in their own garden back home, only a much smaller version.

'A fig tree!' exclaimed her father. 'Now that is what I call…'

'Yes?'

'Timely.'

Rocio shrugged. Well, timely may not be the word she would have chosen, but it certainly wasn't the worse thing to say.

'Yes, Papa – it's timely.'

They both put their bags down and sat beneath the shade of the large fig tree. The lush patch of land was surrounded by palm trees that enclosed it and gave shelter. Within the shade Rocio experienced an air of tranquility. She closed her eyes. She had the sensation she could be anywhere, even back home in her parent's house with the neighbor's cat Neko prowling around the pines. Rocio felt she was within her own world, with her at the center and the circumference nowhere and…and then…there was nothing. Rocio was asleep.

Her father Luis Rodriguez Rodriguez soon followed, for sleep was a timely thing.

The sun had reached its zenith when they awoke.

'We've slept so long, I can't believe it,' said Rocio stretching out her arms.

Her father stood up and shook the sleep off his limbs. 'And we've lost a lot of time as well. We didn't plan for such a long siesta.'

A woman stepped forward from the line of palm trees. 'You've lost no such thing. You cannot lose what you don't have. Time is not yours, and there's always enough if you know how to use it.'

Luis Rodriguez Rodriguez and Rocio jumped around to face a tall, thin woman.

'You don't have to say anything. The look of surprise on your face says it all. A woman out here in the middle of nowhere? I know, it's almost as absurd as a father and his daughter wandering down a path blindly. Take my word for it, from where I'm standing you two are the most surprising thing here.'

The woman stepped into the softened gaze of the sun. Her long, flowing hair was completely grey, and she wore gently fitting cotton slacks. The lady pulled her hair together and fastened it back into a pony-tail. 'Damn long hair. If I don't pull it back it will start to grow around the trees.'

Rocio didn't know whether to smile or…

'You can close your mouth now, young lady. It's rude to stare.'

'Sorry, I…'

'I know. I'm not what you were expecting. That's okay, I get it all the time.'

Luis Rodriguez Rodriguez made a low cough. 'Señora, it's not that we were expecting anything, but…'

'But, yeah, what you weren't expecting just happened to turn up. Right?'

Luis Rodriguez Rodriguez stammered. The lady waved him away with a brush of her hand.

'Hey, get over it. You don't need to bring your social norms and niceties here. Just be yourselves.'

Cool, thought Rocio.

The lady offered Luis Rodriguez Rodriguez and Rocio shelter to rest. She told them to just call her the Keeper, for that was what she was – the Keeper of the Fig Tree. Behind the row of palm trees that surrounded the lush grass and its fig tree stood a low one-story mud brick building. The main entrance led to several rooms on both sides. The rough brick floor was strewn with colored rugs. Everything in the house was simple, as if there only to serve a function. All the shelves and storage spaces were made from local clay mud. There were no tables or chairs. Rocio and her father soon discovered that the floor was the most used space. So that was where they sat down.

They shared a few figs, dates, dried nuts, and some water. Rocio was curious about this so-called Keeper. It was obvious from the way she moved that she had elegance and composure. Rocio also recognized that her directness in speech concealed an educated mind. The lady seemed strangely out of place and yet so comfortable in her space. Rocio tried to guess her age. She suspected she was slightly older than her father. But she also knew that you couldn't always trust the deceptive look of a head of grey hair.

The Keeper kept quiet. She expected that the new guests would be discreetly trying to observe her. Yet to her their attempts were far from discreet. She could feel their gaze upon her like gilded moonbeams. But for now, she was content not to speak. There would be time enough for that.

The oil lamp burned and illuminated the earthiness of the mud brick walls. The darkness had enclosed around them quickly. The hours of night seemed to bring comfort to the small house. Luis Rodriguez Rodriguez sensed that stillness and silence were the two guardians of the place. Rocio must have recognized it too for she chose not to speak. Father and daughter listened to the sounds that moved softly through the still night, as unspoken whispers across silent seas.

Night creatures called out, singing to the dark expanse as if saying *we are here…we are here*. Each tiny voice wanting to declare the beating of their little hearts to the world. And time listened, listened, listened…

It was time to awaken to a new day. Luis Rodriguez Rodriguez and Rocio found a simple breakfast waiting for them outside their rooms. Outside, the Keeper was sitting in meditation under the fig tree. Rocio was intrigued. Curiosity had burrowed into her during the night and laid its eggs. As quietly as she could she stepped over to the fig tree and sat down under its shade. She closed her eyes and told herself to find the timeless place where familiar voices dwell as old friends.

When she opened her eyes again she found a few fresh figs in front of her.

'Try them, you won't get fresher ones. The tree has offered them to you.' The Keeper squeezed a fig and ate its contents. Rocio tried to do the same, with sticky results.

'Why are you here?'

The Keeper tried to hold back a laugh. 'I could ask the same of you. What you really mean to say is – what's my story?' The older lady nodded towards Rocio's father who was a short way off. 'Let him come. Then we have the story.'

Luis Rodriguez Rodriguez came strolling up to the fig tree and sat down to join his daughter. 'You have a lovely place here.' He popped another fresh fig into his mouth and munched contentedly.

'It's not my place, but you are welcome. Here is a place of refreshment. It is for people traveling on their paths.' The Keeper gave a knowing look. 'There are more people on their way than you realize. They each have their task.'

'Yes, yes, I understand,' said Luis Rodriguez Rodriguez.

'Do you?'

'I have my task too. And if I do everything else but not this, then…'

'Yes, yes, I know the way it goes.' The Keeper interrupted with a casual wave of her hand. 'Now that you've both eaten of the figs you must listen to my story. No one leaves refreshed from here without a story. It would be like entering an eye clinic and leaving blind.' The Keeper smiled reassuringly.

A gentle breeze blew through the lush glade and brushed the faces of each person as if to say, *I the wind move amongst you…I have my task too…*

'And like most stories,' said the Keeper, 'it all started with a dream. One night long, long ago I was awakened in my dream. When I opened my eyes, I saw a huge shadow standing by the side of my bed. I instinctively knew, with the whole of my being, that this apparition was the Angel of Death. It had come to claim me; to rid me of my mortal body. I could feel my heart pound so deeply I thought I would die there and then of a heart attack. The Angel of Death began to move away from the bed and I was compelled to follow it, my body moving beyond my volition as if bewitched. Yet although my body obeyed, my mind – my will – protested against this untimely invasion. It took great inner strength but finally I was able to give power to my voice. 'I'm not ready to leave,' I managed to say. I begged again. I pleaded to remain. The Angel of Death stopped and turned to look at me. A hooded darkness stared at me from the infinite depths. The figure did not move. 'Let me stay here and I will give you half of my fortune.' You do not know this, but I was an extremely wealthy person. I was the CEO of a large corporation and my family was amongst the wealthiest. I was used to getting my own way, and usually by paying for it. Yet the apparition shook its hooded head. I was desperate now. I could feel my whole body was covered in sweat. I felt sticky and sick, as if death was beginning to creep over me. 'I will give you all my fortune – everything. Let me remain!' I was crying now, like a hopeless child. Again, the apparition shook its head, yet said nothing. 'I will give you all of my fortune for just one day more!' Again, nothing. 'I will give you everything I have in this world for just one hour more!' I was down on one knee. 'For one minute more…!!' Death was drinking into me and hollowing me out. 'Oh, for the love, for just a few seconds more!'

This time the apparition appeared to nod. I had a few seconds reprieve, and in that moment, I felt an immensity of gratitude for life. Life was the most bountiful of gifts. For just a few seconds more it tasted as sweet as nectar. I ran to my desk and scribbled a few words…whatever I could within those remaining precious few seconds. Then…then I remember no more.'

'What happened next?' asked Rocio with a tremble in her voice.

'Then I awoke with the sun streaming through the crack in

my curtains. I cannot tell you how relieved I felt. I laughed hysterically. It had all been a dream. What a fool I had been. Then I felt anger swell up within me. How dare they try this on, making me beg in my own dreams! That was a sacred realm only for me. It was the one place I knew I had no control in, and the fact that they had violated my vulnerable space made me feel so angry. I got out of bed and stomped through into the other room. And it was then that I saw it…'

The Keeper paused, her face ashen.

'Yes? What did you see?'

'The note I had left,' replied the Keeper softly.

Rocio's eyes widened, as did her father's.

'There it was, as plain as plain sight.'

Rocio leaned forward. 'And…what did it say?' She clutched her father's hand instinctively.

The Keeper's face looked distant as if remembering back to some long, far-flung event that the mind had tried to re-clothe. 'The note was a hasty scribble. It read: *Don't waste your time. My whole fortune could not buy me more than a few seconds… don't waste yours…*' The Keeper looked up into the faces of Rocio and her father. 'And that's where the note ended. I was out of time.'

The three figures sat still, out of time, beneath the shade of the large fig tree.

'I realized then that there was no time to waste,' continued the Keeper; 'that my old life was holding me captive. I was held tightly in place by all my beliefs, and together with my sense of time they had become my jailor. I used to think I was in possession of my fate; that I was in control of all that I did and all that would happen to me. I had created my own disillusioned sense of life and time, and it had wound around me like a darkened thread. After this dream though the thread began to disintegrate, leaving a space where new possibilities could enter. And through this space the gracious infinite peered in. I saw my infinite self. I was looking back at me. I felt then so small in this world. Outside of this trap I sensed everything was so vast. Outside of time there is everything. Here, we are bound by the restrictions we place upon ourselves.'

There was another long pause as Luis Rodriguez Rodriguez and Rocio absorbed what the Keeper had just said.
'And what about us?' Rocio wasn't exactly sure what she wanted to say.
'And do we have time for our task – for the lighthouse?' asked her father.
The Keeper nodded thoughtfully. 'It seems you have already begun to carve out your own path of time. Now it is to be seen how this world, this universe, will respond to you.'
'Are we taking too much time for our journey?' asked Rocio.
'The journey itself should indicate its necessary time. You cannot force this. Time is needed for such things. Otherwise

you will arrive at your destination not suitably prepared. You cannot just turn up for such tasks. You will never reach your destination if you are on the other road. You have to know, to learn, *how to arrive.*'

'And sometimes,' added Luis Rodriguez Rodriguez, 'meetings happen that assist the journey. They give us something to take away, don't they?'

'There are such meetings,' agreed the Keeper. 'Our meeting here will have unforeseen consequences, for all of us. None shall leave here unaffected. None shall leave here unmoved by this encounter. Each moment creates new possibilities, and this carries with us wherever we go. We accumulate possibilities that within the infinite are still infinitesimal drops. These drops mark our lives as we drink from one pool, then the other, and countless pools that make up the grand ocean.' The Keeper stood up. 'Take some rest and refreshment here, for time has granted you grace. Later you shall continue on your way. I'll see you again soon. Now I need to attend to other matters. Oh, and bear in mind that the importance of something is often in inverse proportion to its appearance.' The Keeper, tall and elegantly poised, walked away from the fig tree.

'What did she mean by that?' Luis Rodriguez Rodriguez looked at his daughter with bewilderment.

Figs, dates, dried fruit and nuts were in abundance. Plenty had been collected and the two travelers had their bags loaded. Rocio went to sit under the fig tree and closed her eyes. She relaxed her body and allowed herself to drift into the spaces inside. Her mind returned to the story of the Keeper. Had it really been true? Had this successful woman really given up everything to come and tend a fig tree in the middle of nowhere? There was something that Rocio couldn't quite grasp; an understanding still out of her reach.

After some time, the Keeper returned. She stood by the fig tree, and then waited. And she waited.

'Erh, I've been thinking,' said Rocio, 'and there's something I...'

'Things only seem absurd to the mind,' interrupted the Keeper. 'You have to stop thinking about them. The mind, the intellect, can only take you so far.'

Rocio looked at her father. 'Well, yes. I mean, who would ever think that a lighthouse in the desert would be a good idea!'

'Exactly,' replied the Keeper. 'And yet you felt something different, didn't you?'

Rocio nodded. 'I just looked into my Papa's eyes...then I knew.'

The Keeper looked deep into Rocio's eyes then abruptly walked off and disappeared beyond the palm trees. Rocio looked at her father. Luis Rodriguez Rodriguez shrugged.

Several moments later a loud shriek was heard. Suddenly, the Keeper jumped out from behind the palm trees, leaping and bounding in the air as if in a frenzy. Wack! Something hit Luis Rodriguez Rodriguez on the head. Then again – wack…and another. Something hit Rocio too. She looked at the floor – dates. The Keeper was throwing dates at them!

'Aghh…!!' The Keeper continued to leap about, and now with her arms waving madly in the air. 'How dare you! How dare you! You come here to steal my figs. Scram from here, you scoundrels…'

The Keeper started throwing more dates at Rocio and her father. Luis Rodriguez Rodriguez staggered back.

'Come on, let's get out of here. She's gone crazy!' Luis Rodriguez Rodriguez grabbed his backpack and passed the other to Rocio. 'Put it on and let's go, now!'

The Keeper started to run towards them yelling and hurling more dates, her face contorted and snarling. 'Yahh…get out of here…you better get going and keep going.'

Rocio knew they could not hang around any longer; there was no more time to waste. She started running with her father close behind her.

'That's right, run! Keep going – and don't look back!'

They left behind the lush glade, and kept on running, trying to put as much space between them and the crazy date-throwing Keeper…

…and they kept on running…

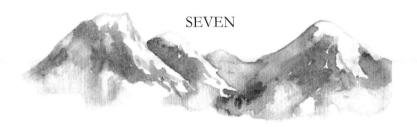

SEVEN

Town of…Erh

…and running until they were so exhausted they had to stop.
They sat down at the side of the road. It was only then that
Rocio realized she still had her hands clenched. When she
finally opened them she found two dates in her right palm.
'I must have caught them,' she muttered to herself.
'What?'
'Oh, nothing. Here, take a date.'
Rocio and her father each popped a date in their mouths and
munched.
'That was strange,' said Luis Rodriguez Rodriguez.
'Well,' said Rocio as she finished her date, 'it could have been
stranger.'
'Mmm…I guess anything can get stranger, so we must thank
our lucky stars for that.'
'Talking of stars, we could do with one to guide us now.'
Luis Rodriguez Rodriguez looked over at his daughter and
again a rush of gratitude washed over him. He started to

laugh. At first just a little, and then more, and soon he was laughing as loud as he ever had before. And as everyone knows, there is nothing more infectious than laughter. Rocio burst out laughing too. The both of them sat there, father and daughter, crying with laughter.

Anyone walking by would have thought that these two unusual travelers had eaten from a crazy cookie, or drank from the well of silliness, or something. It was all a bizarre combination – dates, stars, being lost, infected with laughter, and the light of gratitude and love. But sometimes the strangest ingredients make for the tastiest stew.

The road lay ahead of them, winding and curving and beckoning them on. When there is not much choice the best thing is not to think about it too much. Since going back was not an option, going forward was. Rocio and her father brushed the laughter from their clothes and let it fall away onto the dusty road. Onwards they walked as the sun followed them overhead, observant and curious as to the passing of events.

Later, as the sun set and went peering over to the other side of the planet, Rocio and her father sat down to watch the stars emerge. All afternoon they had been walking in a downward direction until they found themselves in a valley. And this was a good thing for the evening was mild instead of a little chilly. The sky was clear above them, unpolluted from city lights. Luis Rodriguez Rodriguez and Rocio sat back upon a grass slope and stared upwards into the heavens. It was as if a veil had been pulled back and a celestial treasure was visible to the human eye.

'So much out there,' whispered Rocio. 'I wish I could reach out and connect with just a little of what's out there. I'm not greedy. I don't want it all. Just the tiniest of touches will do.' Luis Rodriguez Rodriguez sighed. 'Aye, so much…there's so much.'

And while the two Rodriguezes were gazing upwards they failed to see that further below them other lights were beginning to shine.

The next morning, after a breakfast of dried fruit and nuts, Rocio and her father saw that just below them, after the bend of the road, stood a small town. Whether or not they wanted to visit it was not a question. There was no going around the town.

As they arrived at the main road that led into town it was obvious that here there was life. People were walking the streets, sitting together and talking, and the place hummed with general activity. It was apparent that the town was not large, and the main road constituted the majority of it. Adobe buildings of various sizes lined the main thoroughfare. The general atmosphere was one of easy-going, no rush, today-is-as-good-as-tomorrow type feeling. Even the birds that glided overhead seemed to be in no particular rush to soar anywhere.

Rocio and her father stopped at a roadside water tap to refill their flasks and refresh themselves. They stood for a few minutes observing the comings and goings of the town. Rocio looked around her, sensing there was something she had yet to pick up.

'That's it,' she said suddenly.

'What's it?'

'Look at the people; they don't look local. They're all pale skinned, some with long hair, a lot of blondes too. It seems more like we're in a European holiday village.'

Luis Rodriguez Rodriguez looked around him and nodded. 'Yeah, you're right – it does!'

'Let's try something out.' Rocio stepped away and hailed a nearby woman. 'Good day!'

'Good day,' the middle-aged woman replied. Her accent had a mild yet distinguishable North American twang.

'Where are we, by the way?'

The woman took a second to think. 'Well, by the way sounds about right.' She was about to move on when Rocio called out again.

'Sorry, but we're not from around here. We're strangers to this town. We just want to know…' Rocio paused.

'We're all strangers here. What do you want to know?'

Rocio's face went blank. 'I'm not sure, really.'

'That's fine then. I'll be going on my way. G'day to you.' The woman walked off as if nothing had happened.

'That's funny.'

Luis Rodriguez Rodriguez looked at this daughter. 'What is?'

'I'm not sure.'

'Let's find some place to sit down and rest,' suggested her father.

People smiled at them as they made their way down the main street of the town. Everyone seemed happy and friendly enough. Perhaps, thought Rocio, they were used to strangers passing through. Finally, they spotted a café where people were sitting, drinking, and watching the world gently meander by. The two travelers found an empty table and sat down. It wasn't long before two glasses of hot steaming tea were placed in front of them. Luis Rodriguez Rodriguez looked at his daughter.

'Well, seems like we don't need to order around here.'

'You don't have to order, man, it's the only thing they serve around here.'

Without being invited a young man with long, braided hair pulled up a chair and sat at their table.

'Sorry?'

'That's okay, dude, I get that you don't get it. But they only have one drink here and it's this sweet, deliiiciousss tea...and man, its good. You know what they say?'

'That tea is good for you?' said Luis Rodriguez Rodriguez.

'No man, or yeah, maybe they do. But like what they also say is that why change the recipe when something works. Yeah, right?'

'Yeah, right.' Luis Rodriguez Rodriguez turned to look at Rocio.

'Yeah, right,' said Rocio.

'Yeah, right. See, you're getting it now. So, who are you guys then?' The young man with his scraggly blond braided hair sipped his tea. His face looked newly tanned as if beneath it was hiding a pale shade from some former life. It wasn't difficult to notice that besides his unkempt scruff of a beard he also had tattoos creeping from under the sleeves of his T-shirt. The T-shirt looked like it had gone through several reincarnations. On the front of it was a faded picture of a blue bottle of wine and a line of text underneath which read: *Blue Nun Appreciation Society – Membership: 1.*

'We're the Rodriguezes,' said Luis Rodriguez Rodriguez with a smile.

The young man nodded as if he understood in some profound way. 'Yeah, that's cool…yeah, the Rodriguezes, sure. I've not met any Rodriguezes before, but I've met purple unicorns, pink dragons, and a blue meerkat.' The young man laughed into his tea as if it was some private in-joke.

'Cool,' said Luis Rodriguez Rodriguez trying to go along with the whole weirdness of the situation.

'Yeah, you both wanna see 'em?'

Luis Rodriguez Rodriguez and Rocio nodded in unison. The

young man then stood up and took off his T-shirt. Underneath, his skinny, sun-tanned body was like an illustrated picture book, filled with everything he had just mentioned: a purple unicorn, a pink dragon, and a blue meerkat. And there were other strange squiggles too, looking like rays of light, triangles, eyes, and what-not. The young man grinned.

'See! You see, don't you?' He turned around and upon his back was an image of what looked like two snakes crawling around and up his spine. 'That's my piece-de-resistance. I call it the Kundalini Fire, man. Get that too? I'm well-fired up, I tell you.'

'Impressive,' said Rocio in a casual tone.

The young man put on his T-shirt and sat down again. 'Yeah, bet you it is.'

'What's your name, young man?'

The guy squinted. 'I ain't so young, dude. I've been around many lifetimes.'

'Okay, then allow me to rephrase. What is your name?'

'Yeah, they call me around here *Third Eye*.' The young man nodded slowly and closed his eyes. 'Yeah, everyone knows me here. We're all brothers…and sisters too,' he added looking over to Rocio.

'Interesting name - Third Eye. Was that always your name?'

'No, dude, back home I was…erh, well, I was called something so, yeah, so 'The System' man, you just know it.'

'Okay, Third Eye…'

'You can just call me TE, man – everyone does around here,'

interrupted TE.

'TE, as in tea?' asked Luis Rodriguez Rodriguez as he lifted up his glass of sweet green tea.

'Yeah, cool eh. How just so apt is that?'

'So apt.'

Luis Rodriguez Rodriguez and TE nodded together.

'Hey, man, why don't I show you around this place? That'd be cool, right? I could be like, erh, like your guide or something. Come on, it's on me!'

Luis Rodriguez Rodriguez and Rocio hardly had time to make a decision, let alone say anything, before TE jumped up out of his chair and picked up one of the backpacks. He put his hand in his pocket and then placed two colored pebbles on the table. 'Tea's on me too,' he said with a grin. Then he strode out with Luis Rodriguez Rodriguez and Rocio hastily following with their other backpack.

'Gonna show you to my place,' called back TE as he marched ahead at a strong pace.

'And what do you call this place – this town?' asked Luis Rodriguez Rodriguez as he tried his best to catch up with TE.

'This town…? Erh…this is the town of…erh…look, that's my place.' TE pointed over to a row of open shop fronts, each one showing different wares. One was selling sweet cakes and similar things; another what looked like handmade objects, trinkets, and ornaments; another had strange, dyed looking clothes; and then…

'A surf shop?' Luis Rodriguez Rodriguez and Rocio stopped

beside TE as all three of them stared at a row of bright and colorful surfboards.

'Yeah, man, aren't they all so beautiful? I mean, they're like my children. That's why I can't sell 'em. You see, it'd be like selling my own family. And you wouldn't do that, right?'

Luis Rodriguez Rodriguez nodded. 'You've got a point.'

'Besides, it's not like there's a huge demand for them around here,' added Rocio with a straight face.

TE jumped back. 'Noo, you're so wrong, dude – *everyone* wants a piece of my surf. They're like golden dolphins in a sea of darkness.' TE made a stroking motion with his hand as if cutting through soft caramel. 'These golden dolphins glide through the dark waters and bring the light, man – they're true lightbringers…'

'But you never sell them?'

'Nope!' TE slapped Luis Rodriguez Rodriguez on the back and stepped into the shop with their backpack.

Rocio gave her father one of her oh-yeah looks. 'Golden dolphins,' she whispered as she walked past.

TE's shop, if one could call it that, was really a workshop where surfboards and partially finished boards were propped up in every available space. Each board seemed to be an experiment in colors; some looking more successful than others. At the back of the shop was a low table and a floor strewn with cushions. TE dropped the backpack down and flopped onto a cushion.

'Wonderful,' said Luis Rodriguez Rodriguez. 'Now that we've seen your lovely surf shop do you think you could show us more of this town? Or, if it's too much trouble we could always be on our way.'

'Trouble, man? There ain't no trouble here. Wanna cup of tea?'

Luis Rodriguez Rodriguez and Rocio shook their heads.

'And why you wanna be going when you just got here? That makes no sense, dude. And where you going to?' TE leaned back on the cushion and rocked his head forward as if listening to some inner tune.

'Ahem.' Luis Rodriguez Rodriguez cleared his throat. 'I actually have a task to do. If I do everything else but not this, then...'

He stopped speaking. For once no one had interrupted him, least of all TE who didn't even appear to be listening.

Luis Rodriguez Rodriguez turned to Rocio. 'I think we better be going...'

'Where?' Rocio had a quizzical look in her eyes, as if her irises had decided to question themselves.

They heard a noise from the front of the shop. Someone had just entered.

'TE! Surf's up, sweet mango!' A young woman with similar braided blonde hair, looking around the same age as TE, came waltzing over. 'Ohhh, guests, sweet. How are you, sweeties?'

TE jumped up from his cushion. 'Hey, Moon, so cool, we got guests. This is...erh...and his...'

'Daughter,' interrupted Rocio.

'Yeah, so right on. It's like this, Moon; they show up and I'm like, yeah, y'know, gotta show these dudes around, right? Next thing you know they wanna see my collection of golden dolphins.'

'Who wouldn't, sweetie?' The young girl turned to Luis Rodriguez Rodriguez and Rocio and blew them both a kiss. 'Love you! I'm Blood Moon, but my friends just call me Moon.' She pointed up into the air. 'Y,know – like that shiny thing up there.'

'Got it,' said Rocio smiling.

Moon clapped her hands. Her face was full of smiles and friendliness, even if her eyes didn't seem to be quite sure where they were supposed to focus.

'Have you shown them around town, TE?'

'I was just about to. It was the next thing on my mind.'

'Don't you worry, sweet mango, let ol' Moon be the shining guide – just like in the old days before the Great Fall.'

Luis Rodriguez Rodriguez scratched his head.

Rocio knew better than to do one of her oh-yeah looks.

The three of them walked down the main street as Moon pointed out how lovely the whole place was. They say that beauty is in the eyes of the beholder, and in this case such a maxim was most suitable. The town appeared to be nothing more than an assortment of mud brick buildings that led to a small open plaza. Across from the plaza square was a larger building.

'That's our Community Hall,' said Moon beaming.

'And that's where the whole community meets?' asked Luis Rodriguez Rodriguez without wanting to sound ironic.

'Oh yeah, sweetie. And you just so have to come and be there – it's a must. Tonight's a great night. We're all gonna get really souled-up. I mean, just so much soul. It's just love; so much love.' Moon appeared to drift off into her own ethers.

Rocio looked around her. 'Where does that path go?' she asked, pointing to a track in the far corner of the plaza.

'What, love? Oh, that path. Nowhere – that's just a road to nowhere. Like, who'd want to go nowhere anyway when everywhere is here, right?'

'Right,' agreed Rocio. This time she did give her father another one of her oh-yeah looks.

'What are you loves doing here, anyway?' Moon looked blankly at her two guests. 'It's okay, you can tell ol' Moon here, she ain't gonna spread it around.'

'I have a task to do.'

Moon looked at Luis Rodriguez Rodriguez. 'What's a task?'

'Well, erh…'

'Never mind,' said Moon with a wave of her hand. 'Whatever it is you need to do, you'll find your answer here. Everyone does, eventually.'

'And where is here, actually?' Rocio couldn't resist asking yet again.

Moon smiled. 'Here is where you find your true self. It's all about looking in here.' She pointed to the left of her chest.

'Your true self, true power – you can change the world.' Moon stared out into space.

'Wait!' Moon was running to catch them up.

Luis Rodriguez Rodriguez and Rocio were walking across the plaza. A few other people were mingling around, but they didn't seem to take any notice of their presence. Luis Rodriguez Rodriguez was beginning to get an odd feeling about the place. He didn't need to say anything to Rocio because, as usual, she was way ahead of him on instinct. They both wanted to check things out for themselves.

The wooden door to the Community Hall was unlocked and they both strolled in without interruption. The place was deserted. Yet strewn across the dusty floor of the large hall were pebbles of many colors – red, green, blue, and white.

'Take as many of the pebbles as you like,' said a voice.

Both Rodriguezes turned around to see a man all dressed in black. And the strange thing about the man was that his appearance was, well, quite normal. The man had short, dark hair and a rather nondescript face. In fact, he could have been mistaken for many people, so generic was his look. The man nodded. 'Take as many of the pebbles as you like,' he repeated.

Just then Moon entered the large hall. 'Ah, loves – there you are!' She took them both by the hand. 'We can be here tonight,

no rush. But you both must be hungry. Let's eat something.'
Moon started to lead them both by the hand out of the hall.

Luis Rodriguez Rodriguez turned around to say something to
the man in black. But no one was there.

Moon took them back to TE's place where they ate some
fruit and bread and drank sweet tea. It was all so delicious.
Afterwards they sat back on the soft cushions and relaxed.
Rocio looked up at some of the colorful surfboards and
imagined them as golden dolphins slicing through the dark
waters, bringing baubles of light and bubbles of grace to
those in need.

Luis Rodriguez Rodriguez was thinking of
constructing a mud brick house and having a special room
for keeping a donkey…a donkey? How did that image get in
there? Then another thought entered his mind.

He leaned over to Rocio. 'I thought I heard a voice which told
me to take as many of the colored pebbles as I like.'

'I think I heard a voice similar to yours,' said Rocio wistfully.

A vision of flying golden dolphins crept over her as she leapt
through an ocean spray.

EIGHT

Blind Elijah

The afternoon had turned out to be a dreamy one. After eating their food all four of them - Luis Rodriguez Rodriguez, Rocio, TE, and Moon – had fallen into a deep siesta. They dreamt of many things which, not surprisingly, had evaporated like hot water into steam upon awakening. Rocio had a vague memory of chewing on some small brown nut-like fruit...but no, that couldn't have been right. Maybe she had mistaken it for sucking on her own tongue. And her father, Luis Rodriguez Rodriguez, thought he had had a dream where he was sitting backwards on some four-legged horse-like creature. Only that it wasn't a horse, it had been smaller, and somewhat hairier. Like his daughter, he brushed the vague image out of his mind as one brushes windblown leaves out of the front door.

Dusk settled over the town as if a giant hand had covered her over. The sunset shimmered a hazy orange with purple streaks, and all around was eerily quiet. If there were birds nesting nearby then they had forgotten their birdsong. Perhaps they had even forgotten how to fly. Life within the town seemed enclosed within its own endless, repeating patterns. And one of these patterns was the evening dance, where everybody jigged and fiddled the night away.

'Come on!' shouted Moon with enthusiastic encouragement. 'You just *have to* come along to our evening get-together. We all dance like happy moonbeams!' said Moon, beaming.
'And the stars surf among us, man – it's dead cool,' added TE with a mighty grin.
Luis Rodriguez Rodriguez and Rocio allowed themselves to be herded along to the Community Hall in the town plaza. By the looks of things, everybody in town had the same destination. A long trail of people shuffled to the hall, some with instruments in their hands and a glassy look in the eyes.
'Do you think…' said Luis Rodriguez Rodriguez, and then he stopped in mid-sentence.
Rocio shrugged. 'I don't know.' She wasn't sure what else to say.

The Community Hall soon filled up. People took their positions without talking as if everything had been done so many times before. TE and Moon guided Rocio and her father over to the side of the hall and they sat down on a row of old wooden chairs. At one end of the hall there was a raised platform where a group of musicians were now forming and arranging themselves. The middle of the hall was left open, presumably to be filled once the music started.

A few strings were plucked, and the people in the room stopped shuffling and pricked up their ears. First one fiddle, and then two started to twang, and a jig melody hit the air. A few people immediately leapt out of their seats and began to gyrate, twirl, and jig-dance in the middle of the room. Rocio noticed that with almost everyone's hair being long, a whole lotta hair was being tossed around as heads swiveled and rocked to the escalating rhythms. A flute soon joined the chorus, and then a couple of tin whistles; then a tambourine, some clappers, a metallic ding-dingy thingy… and soon a whirlwind of jigging music was energizing the hall. It looked as if people were spontaneously jumping out of their seats when the mood took them and joining in with the whirly gig.

Luis Rodriguez Rodriguez and Rocio looked at each other. Was this even real? Or did the real even come into it? Rocio looked over to the group of musicians and saw that one of the fiddlers, a girl even younger than herself, had a tiny baby strapped to her back. As the young girl fiddled and hopped from foot to foot, the tiny baby was jiggled around in its straps. And yet the baby slept, oblivious to all that was going on around it. Suddenly TE grabbed Rocio by the hand. 'Come on!' he shouted, 'let's boogie like you've never boogied before, girl!' Rocio didn't have time to stop herself as she was hurled into the thriving mix of long-haired whirly-giggers. At the same time Moon reached out for Luis Rodriguez Rodriguez and pulled him up by the arm. 'You too, old timer!' Moon then hurled the both of them into the throng.

The music kept on playing, reaching crescendo after crescendo, jiving up and down as if navigating the shamanic byways of other realms. Rocio and her father danced the whole night without once stopping for rest. Or, if they had stopped, then they didn't remember it. They were caught in a maelstrom of music; a gigantic swirl of jigs and twirls, turns and twists, and fiddle-grooves.

'That was groovy, man!' declared TE as he finally sat down exhausted upon one of the chairs. Rocio slumped down beside him, and her father and Moon soon followed. Rocio's face was drenched in sweat. She turned to look at her father, and saw the same exhausted, sweat-drenched face staring back at her. And there was something else too. A dreaminess in the eyes that gave a haunted look. It was if the eyes were turning inward on the hunt for some lost thread of memory, or hope.

Rocio felt a jolt in the pit of her stomach, and something deep within her stirred. Just then she happened to glance across the hall and noticed a dark figure opposite. It was a man dressed all in black, and something about him seemed vaguely familiar. It was as if she thought she knew him or had known him; or something along those lines. But now her own lines were blurred and no longer lead in a straight direction. Rocio wiped the sweat from her eyes and looked again. Yes, the man was still there. He appeared to be staring directly at her. She nudged her father and pointed to the other side of the hall. Luis Rodriguez Rodriguez squinted and frowned. There was no man in black; only a row of exuberantly exhausted dancers. And the baby strapped to the back of the young fiddler still slept, as if babies were immune to the musical drug.

Soon everyone slept. The whole town slipped out of the world's space and into the corner of its own imaginings.

Morning crept in stealthily as if on quiet tip-toe. Luis Rodriguez Rodriguez let out a low moan. Rocio grabbed her face and tried to shake the cloudiness from her head. No one had drunk anything during the night, and yet Rocio's head still felt heavy. They were both lying on cushions at the back of TE's surf shop. Rocio groggily glanced over to her father as a throb pulsed in her chest. She felt as if she was missing something…as if, as if she could do all the things in the world yet if there was one thing she did not do, then…

'Sleepy heads, rise and shine!' The bright, cheery voice of Moon radiated to the back of the shop as she came marching in. TE was in tow behind her, shuffling casually and twisting a long dread of hair around his finger. 'Time for breakfast, come on!'

Luis Rodriguez Rodriguez pulled himself up and scratched his cheek. Where was he again? Ah yes, in TE's shop in the town of…erh…which town?

Shortly they were both following Moon and TE down the main street and into a café for breakfast. They thought the café looked somehow familiar yet by now they had already forgotten that it was the same café where they had first met TE. But days were now like pancakes – flattened and soon gone.

'Pancakes, anyone? Dude, they're so deliciously delicious here.' TE smacked his lips and playfully slapped his stubbly cheeks with both hands.

'I'll order us a super-hyper mixed breakfast.' Moon wandered off and left the three of them sitting at the table, staring into space.

As Rocio's eyes slowly focused she saw a figure dressed in black sitting at a corner table. And he was observing them. Rocio nudged her father. 'Look, it's him again.'

Luis Rodriguez Rodriguez squinted. 'Yes…yes…' He paused as if thinking, as if trying to dredge up from the depths some flicker of memory as a fisherman hopes for the day's big fish. 'Big fish, little fish, cardboard box…' he mumbled to himself.

'What?!'

'Nothing…just a game, a…that's it…the man who offered

the colored pebbles!'

Rocio's eyes lit up in recognition. She remembered now too.

Moon sat down at the table with a dreamy smile on her face. 'You're gonna love it here. Everyone does. In fact, no one ever wants to leave, it's so dreamy here!'

'Who's that man over there?' Rocio pointed to the man in black.

'Oh, that's Elijah,' said Moon with a casual wave of her hand. 'Don't worry about him, he won't bother you. He bothers nobody – he's blind.'

'Blind?!'

Moon and TE nodded in unison, as if someone had rocked their chairs at the same time.

'Yeah, that's Elijah, the blind dude,' said TE. 'He came here shortly after we arrived. As soon as we saw him we knew that he was blind. We weren't the only ones, everyone else saw it too. He's totally blind. But man, we totally accepted him here. He doesn't participate and contributes nothing to the community, but like, dude, we kind of tolerate his presence, if you know what I mean. But, y'know, we're cool about it. We let him be.'

'And how does he take care of himself?'

Moon looked at Rocio and shrugged. 'How should we know? We don't interfere, we just let him be. As TE said, we're cool and leave him alone. Peace to all brothers and sisters. Ain't that so?'

TE nodded. 'Right on, right on.'

If he's totally blind, why does he keep staring at us? wondered Rocio as she munched on the sweet pancakes and sipped the sugary minted tea. Moon let the honey dribble down her chin while TE slurped and made noises as he ate.

TE gave Luis Rodriguez Rodriguez a playful slap on the back. 'Hey bro, you look like you could seriously do with some meditation, pure ashram style. Come on, after this we'll take you both for some far-out mind-melding, meet the universe, cosmic mother type of thing. It'll blast you. Heaven's so close man I can feel it in my fingertips.'

'Holy Cosmic Love,' added Moon.

'Thanks, but I think we'll go for a walk.'

Rocio nodded in agreement with her father while the blind man Elijah kept a close watch.

'Suit yourselves.'

Luis Rodriguez Rodriguez and Rocio stood on the corner of the main street looking at a row of half a dozen people. They were seated on the floor with their heads turned to the sky. They had been watching them for several minutes. No one had moved. With eyes wide open they continued to stare upwards.

'They're sun-gazing,' said a voice.

'What?' Luis Rodriguez Rodriguez and Rocio both turned around. It was the blind man, Elijah.

'They think that by staring at the sun every day they won't need to eat food.' The man in black clicked his tongue. 'It's enough to make you go blind!'

'How do you know?' asked Rocio.

Elijah smiled. 'Because they're looking up at the sun. It's called sun-gazing.'

'Yes…but, but,' stammered Rocio. 'I mean, how do you know what they're doing if you're blind?'

Elijah chuckled gently and shook his head. 'I can see far better than you can, believe me!' he said finally. Rocio's face went blank.

'Oh, so you're not blind then?' asked her father.

'I've got the best eyes in this whole town. It's everyone else who is blind.'

'So, so…' This time it was Luis Rodriguez Rodriguez who stammered.

'So why are you here then?' interrupted Rocio.

'I could ask the same question of you,' the man replied. 'But the short answer is that it's more a case of the blind leading the naked.'

'And who's naked?' As soon as Rocio had asked the question she knew. Her cheeks blushed.

Elijah gave a sympathetic smile. 'It's alright, it happens to everyone.'

'What does?' From the look on Luis Rodriguez Rodriguez's

face it was obvious he was missing the conversation. Elijah placed a hand on his shoulder.

'Everyone in this town thinks they're fully clothed in their own *right on* ways about the world.' Elijah smiled again, and Rocio felt a genuine sincerity in the man whom everyone else thought was blind. 'But they're only clothed in their own delusions – and this makes them forget everything else. Look…' Elijah made a sweep of his hand around the town. 'Everyone came here seeking to escape. And escape they did – but only from themselves. But you two were only passing through. You don't belong here. And you must leave as soon as possible.'

'Leave for what, and where?' A blank look had returned to the face of Luis Rodriguez Rodriguez.

Elijah nodded. 'It has already begun, but it is not yet too late. Come with me.'

Luis Rodriguez Rodriguez and Rocio followed Elijah down a side street and into a one-story building. They entered a front room and Elijah motioned for them to sit down on an old divan. In the middle of the room was a low table and upon it was a ceramic bowl filled with pebbles of many different colors – there were red, green, blue, and white.

'Take as many of the pebbles as you like,' said Elijah gently.

Rocio reached forward first and took three colored pebbles in her hands. Then her father reached out and took two.

'Hold them tightly in your hands.'

Rocio and her father curled their hands into fists and squeezed tightly. Rocio thought she could feel a tingling sensation run through her hand. Her father said nothing, but his eyes were beginning to twinkle like of old.

'Open your hands again,' said Elijah after a short time.

They both uncurled their fists and stared at what was lying in their palms. In both their hands the colored pebbles had changed into small, brown looking soft wrinkled pebbles.

'Strange pebbles,' mumbled Luis Rodriguez Rodriguez.

Elijah laughed. 'Pop them into your mouth and eat them. They're not pebbles!'

Not long after a look of unfolding realization slowly appeared upon both their faces.

'Mmm…dates,' said Rocio with a full mouth.

'Donkeys,' added her father.

'Donkeys?' Rocio pulled a face.

'Dates?' Luis Rodriguez Rodriguez tilted his head. Then it hit them both at the same time.

'Nash!'

'The Keeper!'

Rocio suddenly remembered the Keeper of the Fig Tree throwing dates at them as she chased them away. And then the Keeper's last words came back to her – 'Keep going – and don't look back!'

Luis Rodriguez Rodriguez had a sudden flash of an image in his mind. He saw Nash with his two donkeys…

…and then for both Luis Rodriguez Rodriguez and his

daughter all that had happened since they had first left home once again returned to them. Luis Rodriguez Rodriguez let out a long sigh.

'How could we have forgotten?!' he said, shaking his head. 'We should have kept going like the Keeper said – oh, we've been so stupid!' This time Rocio blushed even deeper than before.

Elijah clapped his hands and jolted Rocio and her father out of their reverie. 'Good, now that's done. Don't blame yourselves. Everyone at some point in their lives succumbs to the fantasy that what they want is the same as what they need. But what people actually need is to find the true light within them.'

'The lighthouse!' shouted Luis Rodriguez Rodriguez and Rocio together.

'It's important that you never, ever forget why it is you came here – and where it is you need to go. This is the only thing that truly gives us sight in our lives. Without this sight we are blind to life, and naked to its whims.'

Luis Rodriguez Rodriguez and Rocio both thanked Elijah for his help.

'And what about you?' asked Rocio. 'Are you going to stay here forever?'

'Forever is a long time, my dear Rocio. I shall be here – wherever *here* is – for as long as people need me; and perhaps a little longer after that. But don't worry about me. I move around far more than you would think. After all, I have good sight.' Elijah smiled. He knew his services were no longer needed.

Their backpacks were fully packed and ready to go. Elijah had given them each a small bundle of food to help them on their way. He had also indicated which road to take in order to leave the town and to continue on their way. With their packs on their backs Luis Rodriguez Rodriguez and his daughter headed for the small track in the far corner of the plaza. It wasn't long before TE and Moon came running after them, as expected.

'Hey dudes,' shouted TE, 'where you going, man? You can't be going like that?'

'Like what?' replied Luis Rodriguez Rodriguez.

'Like, just like *that*, man!'

'Hey lovvies, the fun's only just starting,' added Moon as she finally caught up with them.

'But we're not going anywhere,' said Luis Rodriguez Rodriguez.

TE and Moon looked at each other as if they didn't understand.

'No, we're only taking the road to nowhere,' added Rocio, as she had been instructed to say by Elijah.

'The road to nowhere?' Moon didn't quite know what to say.

'Sure,' said Luis Rodriguez Rodriguez in a reassuring voice.

'And since we're only taking to road to nowhere then we can't be going *anywhere* – can we?'

TE scratched his chin. 'Well, erh…' He looked over at Moon

who just stared back at him with a blank look.

'Well, then, that's settled. Got to be going nowhere.' Luis Rodriguez Rodriguez waved.

'Yes, see you both nowhere soon!' said Rocio with a cheery smile. And off she walked with her father, leaving behind a speechless TE and Moon.

They took the track that lead away from the plaza, and away from the town of…well, whatever it was called.

'In the kingdom of the blind…' said Luis Rodriguez Rodriguez in a low voice.

'The one-eyed girl is queen,' finished Rocio, and took her father's hand.

NINE

The Custodians

They had been told to follow the track out of town and to keep going for over half a day's walk. They would then, Elijah had told them, come upon a small shrine where they could rest for the evening. Elijah had also warned them to keep their eyes in their heads and their tongues firmly in their cheeks – whatever that meant. Luis Rodriguez Rodriguez and Rocio were just both glad to be back on the road again and, more importantly, to have their vision of the lighthouse clearly in sight.

'Who would have thought that building a lighthouse would be so tricky?'

Luis Rodriguez Rodriguez agreed with his daughter. 'But we haven't even started yet. We have to arrive first. We're still on the first stage!' he added.

'Exactly, getting to the place where you can start is so tricky. Next time can we please start from the second stage first?'

Luis Rodriguez Rodriguez laughed. Sometimes his daughter was so smart he wondered why she didn't write joke books for a living.

The sun was high in the sky, having the whole blue canopy for itself. Not even a cloud dared to drift idly by in front of the sun's magnificent glare. Rocio looked into the sky and smiled to herself. She was glad not to be sun-gazing. A person could go blind doing that!

For most of the day father and daughter walked in silence. There was no need to talk. And when there is no need there is no compulsion. Each was content and comfortable just to enjoy the other's presence. They watched the road in front of them unfold with multitudinous color and shades.

Late in the day, as predicted, they saw a gleaming white shrine in the distance. It appeared to be a domed building perched on a slightly raised platform with columns. The building rose up to greet them as they neared.

'Looks like we've found our shelter for the evening.'

Rocio looked at her father but preferred not to say anything and to leave any judgment for later. After all, hadn't Elijah told them to keep their tongues firmly in their cheeks?

As they approached the shrine they noticed that two figures were seated on the floor besides the columns. The figures neither moved nor showed any sign of recognizing their approach. Only when they were at the foot of the steps did they realize that both figures were holy men in silent meditation.

'Should we disturb them?'

Rocio shook her head.

'But it's rude not to introduce ourselves.'

Rocio sighed. 'You're so European, father. It'd be even ruder to disturb them when they're meditating.'

They looked at the two men. One of them was old, with a long, white beard. The other was younger with a shorter, dark beard. Both were wrapped in what appeared to be a single white sheet.

'They sure do look holy,' whispered Luis Rodriguez Rodriguez. 'What should we do then – tiptoe past them?' Rocio caught a sparkle in her father's eyes which made her laugh out loud.

Suddenly the younger of the two holy men opened his eyes.

'Greetings, travelers! Welcome to this Abode of Spring. I am Anwar, Custodian of this shrine. I am humbly at your service.'

The older man popped open one of his eyes. Then he opened the other and spread his arms wide, palms up. A huge smile appeared on his white-bearded face.

'May you be favored in the eyes and heart of our Lord. I am Father Nuri, Custodian of this shrine. May your coming be auspicious.'

'And I am Luis Rodriguez Rodriguez,' said Luis Rodriguez Rodriguez. 'And this is my daughter, Rocio.'

Rocio smiled and held up her hand. 'Hi.'

'Ah, Rocio, Rocio, the name does flow like holy water,' replied the older man, Father Nuri.

'It does roll off the tongue like perfumed nectar,' added the younger man, Anwar.

'Actually,' said Rocio, 'it means the morning dew.'

Father Nuri threw up his hands. 'Ah, how auspicious it is.'

'The very truth of it,' added Anwar.

Rocio shrugged. She thought it best not to say anything else. Like the time she was called to the headmaster's office as a young girl at school. She had been admonished for pulling the hair of one of the boys in her class and calling him *stinky pinky*. She knew that anything she said to the headmaster would only make the situation worse. When something is self-explanatory, she reasoned, then there's no use to add extra words to the situation.

Luis Rodriguez Rodriguez and Rocio smiled and said nothing. Father Nuri tugged on his long, white beard. 'Mmm, and which road did your good feet take to bring you here?'

'The one back there,' said Luis Rodriguez Rodriguez, pointing over his shoulder with his thumb.

'Indeed, the road less traveled by. And which has made all the difference, no doubt?'

'No doubt about it,' added Anwar. 'It's as clear as holy water in a crystal glass.' Anwar looked at Father Nuri, who nodded.

Luis Rodriguez Rodriguez cleared his thought. 'Gentlemen. My road is my journey. Destiny is my way ahead.'

'Destiny?' replied Anwar and Father Nuri.

'Indeed. If I do everything else but not this, then…'

'Yes, yes, that may well be the case,' interrupted Father Nuri, 'but your destiny is here, now.'

Anwar nodded. 'It is destiny that brought you here to us – it can be no other. Destiny moves in all of us like a rapid river.'

'A torrent,' added Father Nuri.

Luis Rodriguez Rodriguez gave Rocio a sideways glance. 'Well, it is true we are here now. May you be so kind as to offer us shelter this evening?'

'This very evening?' Father Nuri looked at Anwar.

'This very night?' asked Anwar.

Luis Rodriguez Rodriguez nodded. 'Tonight.'

Father Nuri and Anwar did not speak.

'Indeed, holy custodians, this very evening and night,' added Rocio. 'The one that comes before tomorrow's dawn.' Rocio smiled at her father.

Father Nuri's face brightened. 'Ah, fair travelers, so this is the seed of your visit?'

'The kernel of your destiny?' added Anwar.

'Yes, dear protectors, and with your holy blessing we ask you for shelter.'

'The fates be upon us,' continued Anwar. 'Your coming is more auspicious than can be known. Blessed be to both your good selves. Destiny does indeed walk in strange circles!'

Father Nuri turned to look at Anwar. 'How so, dear brother?'

'Is not this very night the Saint Eve of our beloved saint that lies here within this very tomb?' Anwar gave his older companion a knowing look.

'Ah, most glorious divinity, so it is! My strong meditations have emptied my mind of such beneficial facts.'

'Strong medications more like,' whispered Rocio under her breath.

The two custodians slowly got up. Father Nuri, despite being of old age, had a mischievous face that could hardly stop expressing a huge smile. Anwar, the younger, was the more serious of the two and appeared to relish the ceremonial trappings.

'Let our hallowed guests rest a while whilst we shall prepare our blessed benediction,' said Anwar as he motioned for them to enter into the antechamber of the shrine.

'Indeed, how ignoble of us not to offer our weary travelers their rest earlier,' added Father Nuri, as he likewise waved them in.

Luis Rodriguez Rodriguez entered the shrine first. Rocio followed. Inside the antechamber the air was cool and refreshing. Lining the walls were benches that beckoned the travelers to rest.

The tranquility of the shrine was welcoming after the last few days. Rocio left her father alone with his thoughts. She was sure he wished for some time to re-gather them and to renew the enigma of his dream. Following a dream is never an easy prospect, and less so when it involves lighthouses and deserts.

Everyone has their dream, Rocio was sure of this. Just as she was sure that cats are cunning, and dogs like to lie in front of log fires. Such things have their place, no matter how crazy, chaotic, or illogical it may seem. Rocio closed her eyes and imagined Neko her neighbor's cat sauntering amidst the pines of her backyard. She smiled to herself. Neko being Neko is no different from Rocio being Rocio. Mineral is mineral, vegetable is vegetable, animal is animal, and human is…

'Rocio?' Her father opened his eyes and looked over.

'Yes, Papa?'

'We're getting closer. I can feel it.'

'To the desert?'

Her father nodded in the shadowy light. 'Yes, Rocio. To the desert of our lighthouse.'

'That's good, Papa. Every journey has to end sometime. Endless journeys never fulfill their destiny.'

Rocio thought she could see her father smile.

'Ah, my dear child,' replied Luis Rodriguez Rodriguez in a tender voice. 'You shine far brighter than any lighthouse ever will. You have a heart filled with true light that glows even when you're sleeping, pouting, or being angry.'

Rocio thought she heard a soft chuckle.

'Then why do we need a lighthouse in the desert if human hearts are to be filled with their true light?'

This time she definitely did hear her father sigh.

'Because people don't know where to look. The guiding light

must first shine from the outside.'

There was a short pause. 'You really did have a good dream that night,' said Rocio in a low whisper.

Three loud claps echoed around the antechamber of the shrine. Luis Rodriguez Rodriguez sat up and gazed at his daughter as if to say — *here we go*!

Anwar entered the domed room carrying incense in one hand and a fan in the other. He chanted a few words under his breath. Father Nuri followed him, finger-cymbals tinkling. They walked together three times around the room, then sat down in the center. Anwar motioned Rocio and her father to join them on the floor. As they sat down they noticed the two custodians daubed in colored paint. The two shrine keepers began nodding their heads back and forth and chanting. Cymbals tinkled. Incense wafted about the room.

To Rocio, the sound of the cymbals was hypnotic, and she enjoyed their effect upon her senses. Since he wasn't going anywhere, Luis Rodriguez Rodriguez decided to relax and allow the chanting and incense to penetrate his being. He preferred this to being chased by a person throwing dates.

Anwar suddenly sprang up from his seated position and started to move in circles around the group. He was making a strange shuffling motion which looked like some kind of odd dance. Rocio raised an eyebrow. The last time she had seen anything close to this was when a boy in her kindergarten class called Billy Barton had tried to dance to the Bee Gees in his socks and underpants. She looked over to her father who still had his eyes closed. Oh well, she thought, it's not a bad place to be. She closed her eyes too and let the chanting, cymbals, and shuffling sounds accompany her as she surfed her own inner seas.

When she opened them again it was dark and silence filled the room. 'I must have fallen asleep,' she quietly whispered.

'You did. *We* did,' came a whisper in return.

'Papa?'

'Sleep now, my dear. Tomorrow the desert beckons us. I can taste its dryness on my tongue.'

'Be careful, Papa. Speaking like that will get you an honorary post as a shrine custodian.'

Her father chuckled. 'From lighthouses to shrines; and I thought I was just a simple architect.'

'Nothing is that simple, Papa. Otherwise, none of us would be here.'

'Maybe you're right. What would a simple architect know, after all?!'

'Goodnight, Papa. Sweet dreams.' As soon as she had said that Rocio regretted it. The last thing she needed right now was another one of her father's strange and sweet dreams. One lighthouse was enough, thank you very much.

Dawn arrived early with a graceful light. Luis Rodriguez Rodriguez was already awake by the time Rocio had opened one of her eyes.

'Why not open the other one?' teased her father.

'Once I open the other one I have to wake up,' replied Rocio with a sleepy voice.

A noise of activity could be heard coming from outside. The two travelers brushed down their clothes and stepped out into an awaiting world.

Father Nuri gave a hearty smile. 'Ah, the pilgrims awaken!'

Anwar looked up from a steaming teapot. 'Ah, our blessed brother is…'

'And sister,' interrupted the elder custodian.

Anwar coughed. 'Ahem, our blessed brother and sister are here to break fast with us. The day is once again auspicious. Come, partake of our humble offerings.'

'Partake so that we may humbly serve,' added Father Nuri with a fiddly wave of his hand.

'Well, I am hungry' replied Luis Rodriguez Rodriguez.

'Thank you, brothers. Your offering is most humble and gracious. We bow to your generosity and offer grace that we may sit with you,' added Rocio.

I must remember to check what she's reading, thought Luis Rodriguez Rodriguez as he gave his daughter a smile.

The four of them ate a simple breakfast of fresh fruit and sweet tea. Rocio couldn't help but notice that the two custodians were swapping eager glances with one another.

'It was an, erh…an *interesting* ceremony yesterday,' said Rocio finally.

Father Nuri clapped his hands together in obvious joy. 'Oh, how so it was!'

Anwar rolled his head with a smile. 'It was a very special and, I may add, unique ceremony that you were allowed to witness. It was a blessing and benediction to the saint of the shrine.'

'Who is…?' interrupted Luis Rodriguez Rodriguez.

Father Nuri looked over at Anwar yet said nothing.

Anwar spread his hands open and bowed. 'We are but humble custodians. Our duty is to serve, not to elaborate unnecessarily.'

'Our duty is to be awake to the needs of pilgrims,' added Father Nuri, and gave Rocio and her father a knowing look.

'Yes, we must be awake and attentive to such needs. Sleep is the brother of death.' Anwar bowed again, this time until his forehead was nearly touching the handle of the metal teapot.

'An hour's contemplation is better than a year's worship,' said Father Nuri.

'Journey even as far as China seeking knowledge,' added Anwar.

'Why do you say that?'

Father Nuri and Anwar both looked at Rocio.

'Say what?' Anwar looked confused.

'About going as far as China seeking knowledge.'

'Because it has always been said,' replied Anwar as if it was the most natural response in the world.

Father Nuri nodded in support. 'I have been around shrines so long, and so have my ancestors, that we cannot know where all the sayings come from. And does it matter?'

'Well, I would have thought so,' responded Rocio. 'They have to *mean* something to people.'

Father Nuri shrugged. 'My dear young child, shrines and their faithful custodians have been here for centuries, not necessarily because of our value or *meaning*, but because people want us. They want to follow a harmless path and feel better; to feel elevated. That, in any case, is what they imagine spirituality to be.'

'But is it true?'

'True? What does it matter if it's true or not. Besides, in a world where there is no light at all, even a false gleam is perhaps worth having.'

Anwar suddenly stood up and spread out his hands high into the air. 'History is our truth, and so shall it always be. Have faith in the eternal rituals and the eternal riches shall be yours!' And just as quickly he sat down again.

'Amen,' echoed Father Nuri nodding his head.

'And do you not feel recharged with the energy of the shrine?' asked Anwar.

Rocio shrugged. 'Well, I do feel like I got a good night's rest.'

'And I feel well rested too,' added her father.

Both the custodians grinned broadly and then in unison said

'Spiritualized.'

'Spiritualized?' A confused look appeared on Rocio's face.

'Sure,' said Anwar, looking sympathetic. 'Our ceremony of last evening helped to clear your chakras and to spin your lotus flowers.'

'Your sacral was most likely blocked from all your days of traveling,' added Father Nuri as he sagely stroked his beard.

'Ahem, well that's good to know.' Luis Rodriguez Rodriguez gave his daughter a quick glance.

'Yes, I suppose so.'

The two custodians clapped their hands together.

'This is auspicious beginnings,' said a delighted Father Nuri.

'You see, this is the truth you seek – you *feel better*. Why worry about the origins of our techniques and knowledge when we know how to clear your energy blockages? Trust in feeling good. Why seek for the unknown when you can feel elevated in the here and now?'

'Aye, the here and now,' repeated Father Nuri.

'I guess some people seek for more,' muttered Rocio quietly under her breath.

'Sorry, sister?'

'Oh, I only said why seek for more?'

'Indeed,' agreed Anwar.

'The long road of seeking is often an escape from life,' added Father Nuri.

'Yes,' agreed Anwar, 'and destiny is often a delusion. We must first work through the ways of this world, through cause and effect. It's the way the world turns. We cannot get from A to Z without first passing through the other letters.'

Rocio pulled a face. 'So, you mean to say that after Alpha comes Beta and not Omega?'

I must check her reading sources when we get back, thought Luis Rodriguez Rodriguez.

Anwar and Father Nuri looked at each other with blank expressions upon their faces.

'My child, do not let such letters and words confuse you. Language is often the device of the devil. We must guard our words well,' said Father Nuri.

'Amen!' echoed Anwar. 'And the devil tries to sneak in when we are unawares. We must be vigilant against all falsities. Trust in that which has always been. Trust in that our history shall be our future.'

'Amen,' echoed Father Nuri. 'My ancestors have been here since the dawn of dawn providing wisdom and shelter, and so shall it always be.'

'Always be,' added Anwar nodding.

Luis Rodriguez Rodriguez stretched his legs and made as if to stand up. 'And talking of shelter, we both thank you greatly for yours, but we must be getting on our way now.'

'Yes,' said Rocio as she too stretched to get up. 'I think a future of shrines is a fine idea, but we have a different destin…'

Rocio paused. 'I mean, we have a different destination.'

The two custodians bowed their heads and chanted something

under their breath. Luis Rodriguez Rodriguez and his daughter collected their bags and made ready to say their farewell.

The two custodians remained seated upon the floor in front of the shrine entrance.

'May you depart richer than when you arrived,' said Father Nuri.

Anwar spread open his hands. 'And perhaps you would care to leave something of value for those who shall come after you?'

Rocio smiled. 'Alright. I would like to leave something which has helped me much in these past years. It is something my mother left to me.'

The faces of both custodians perked up.

'The importance of something is in inverse proportion to its attractiveness,' said Rocio. 'This is the wisdom my mother left me.'

A frown rippled across the face of Anwar and Father Nuri. Perhaps it wasn't the thing of value they had been expecting. But then again, things of real value often come at times and in ways least expected.

'Come on, Papa, time to hit the road. The desert beckons!'

'But, but...are you sure you wish to leave us like this? said Anwar, almost sulkily.

'The caravan moves on,' replied Rocio with a smile.

Father Nuri chuckled quietly to himself.

That's my girl, thought Luis Rodriguez Rodriguez. *I knew the journey would do her good.* He stretched out his arms. Yes, it was a fine day to be moving on. The desert does indeed beckon…

TEN

The Hadji

Sometimes a road is a road. Other times it is something more. After all, not just any road is a journey. And not every road will lead a person to their destination. No, roads are often highly simplified in peoples' minds; which is perhaps why people take the wrong roads, or they take many roads that go nowhere. Or maybe, even maybe, a person takes a road that is not a road at all but something completely different. Yet let it be known that in truth, there is only one *real* road for any one person to take – and that road *will* make all the difference.

For Luis Rodriguez Rodriguez and his daughter Rocio the road they had taken so many days before seemed like it was turning out to be a long and strange road indeed. To be fair, it wasn't a long road in terms of length, as some roads can be longer than all the winding paths in the world placed together. But it was long in their minds, which meant it was longer than their expectations. This is not saying much since expectations are fickle things anyway, and usually are up to no good. But in terms of strange – yes, it was turning out to be that.

Rocio looked down at the dusty road beneath her feet. 'It seems to be getting sandier. We must be nearing the desert.' Her father nodded. 'Yes, the taste is getting stronger on my tongue.'

'Maybe what you're trying to say, Papa, is that you feel the taste of the desert getting stronger in your heart.' Rocio smiled to herself. She knew that men, especially older men like her own father, preferred to cover up emotions with references to other senses – like taste on tongues, for instance.

The insight was not lost on Luis Rodriguez Rodriguez. He turned to give his daughter one of his special 'Papa' smiles.

The road was now gradually becoming less of a road and more of a sandy track. Along its sides were rows of palm trees, standing tall as if singing their songs to far away sand dunes. It is said that all creatures of the desert communicate to each other. The desert has long been known to be a world within itself, where other laws operate. Laws unbeknown to the rest of the non-desert world. As Rocio was thinking about the world of the desert a thought suddenly came into her mind.

'Papa?'

'Uh-huh.'

'When we get to the edge of the desert, what are we going to do?'

'What do you mean?'

'Well, we'll be at the edge of the desert, right?'

'Sure.'

'And we'll be wanting to get into the desert, I presume?'

'Yes, we'll need to get into the desert. There's no point building a desert lighthouse at the edge of a desert. Who'd want that?'

'That's what I thought.' Rocio stopped, pulled out her flask of water and took a drink. 'So, are we just going to walk straight into the desert, just like that?'

Luis Rodriguez Rodriguez looked confused. 'I don't get what you're saying, my dear.'

'Well, that's just it, Papa. You have an architect's mind, and now you've gone and mixed it up with your special-dream mind. And somewhere along the way the *actual-actual* part of your mind took a holiday.'

Her father frowned. 'The *actual-actual* part of my mind?'

Rocio gave one of her daughterly sighs. 'Sure, Papa, the how-actually-are-we-going-to-walk-through-the-desert part of the plan.'

Luis Rodriguez Rodriguez broke out into a smile. 'Oh, that's easy. I brought you along to work that out. That's your part!'

Rocio pouted. It was not what she was expecting to hear.

Father and daughter sat down to take a rest and a drink. They sat beneath the cool shade of a palm tree. Although both were wearing head protection – Rocio her sun hat and her father his blue cotton scarf — they were both sweating. Sun and heat penetrate in different ways. The rays of the sun are direct and come at you with a full-on glare. Heat, on the other hand, is more indirect and seeps into every nook and cranny of the body.

'And the sand, too,' murmured Rocio to herself, 'is getting in everywhere. I feel like it's clinging to me. Aghh…'

Luis Rodriguez Rodriguez gave his daughter a sympathetic look. 'I know; we're not in our comfort zone now. But that's the whole point of traveling. We're experiencing ourselves in other zones.'

'Fine if you're a parking enforcement officer. I'm not sure I'm okay with all these zones!'

'My dear, one does not reach a destination without…'

'Papa!' interrupted Rocio. 'I love you, but could we do without all the wise old sayings, for just this once? I mean, all this destination stuff is fine when you're sitting at home reading a book. It's not the same where you're sitting at the edge of an actual desert!'

Luis Rodriguez Rodriguez nodded and stroked his moustache with his thumb and forefinger. He knew his daughter had a point. A very good point it was too.

And that was when Rocio spotted the wall.

She was somewhat surprised with herself that she had not spotted it earlier. After all, walls were not the type of things that easily hid themselves. On the contrary, walls were often the very things that wanted to be visible, as if showing how one thing can be separated from another.

If there's one wall, then there must be another, thought Rocio. It seemed highly unlikely that one solitary wall would be standing near to the edge of a desert. It seemed reasonable that a wall meant another wall, and then another, until finally you got not walls but a building. And a building was something totally different than just a wall. And this would be useful right now, because it signified so many more things.

'You just have to look for the signs,' said Rocio aloud, both to herself and her father.

Rocio was more right than she may have realized. That's because signs are everywhere and have helped the world go around for many a long time. Only that most signs do not have a sign attached to them which says *This is a Sign*, so most people do not recognize them as such. But in this case, a sign it was.

As they neared the wall they saw that what they thought was a wall was in fact one side of a walled enclosure which had a large opening on the other side. Rocio felt mildly pleased with herself for guessing that they would find more than just a wall. I say 'mildly pleased,' for anything else would have been too much, too soon, considering that the two Rodriguezes still had a desert to cross.

A large bird with outstretched wings flew low overhead. It seemed to Rocio that it was watching them carefully. It glided effortlessly and circled several times before flying away. The black dot in the blue sky disappeared from sight. It was then that Rocio realized that not only could they be in the middle of nowhere but that they actually were in the middle of nowhere. And for the first time Rocio felt vulnerable. Can dreams be dangerous? she asked herself.

Luis Rodriguez Rodriguez rested a hand upon his daughter's shoulder.

'Let's go in. We've come this far. Four walls are neither going to stop us or harm us,' he said, as if reading his daughter's mind.

Rocio nodded. You can't stand outside of walls forever, she thought.

They entered the large, walled enclosure as the sweat rolled off their foreheads and dropped onto the sandy floor. If it wasn't for the eerie silence Rocio imagined they could have been on some film set. It was as if she had seen a place like this in a thousand movies. At the same time she had never *really* seen such a place. Often, she thought, reality and unreality are like the same thing.

'We could be anywhere and nowhere,' said Luis Rodriguez Rodriguez softly.

They were in the middle of a large courtyard with doors leading off at regular intervals in each wall. At the far wall a faded-colored canopy was overhanging one of the doorways. Father and daughter looked at each other without saying a word, and both instinctively moved forward in the direction of the far wall. As they got closer to the canopy they felt something swoop fast and low over their heads. They then heard a fluttering as a largish bird, with a sharp, pointed beak came to rest on a wooden perch beneath the canopy. As they were about to move past its perch the bird gave out a large squawk. For a few seconds all three sets of eyes looked at one another. Luis Rodriguez Rodriguez put his right foot forward and the bird squawked again, this time even louder.

'Who goes there?'
Luis Rodriguez Rodriguez and his daughter both looked at each other. Did the bird just…?
Another loud squawk. 'Who goes there? State your purpose.'
Rocio shrugged. She didn't want to say anything. A thought in the back of her mind told her that she certainly hadn't gone to university to end up talking with birds. She gave her father a coy smile.
Luis Rodriguez Rodriguez stroked the sweat off his moustache.

'Ahem. My name is Luis Rodriguez Rodriguez,' he said in a loud and clear voice, 'and this is my daughter, Rocio.'

The bird squawked again. 'And your purpose, Luis Rodriguez Rodriguez?'

'My purpose – *our* purpose – is to seek a place in the desert where we can build a lighthouse.'

Squawk. 'A lighthouse in the desert, you say?'

'Well, yes.'

'Now that *is* interesting.' Squawk.

'I'm glad you think so, not many people think…'

Rocio interrupted her father by nudging him with her elbow. Luis Rodriguez Rodriguez looked up and noticed a tall figure in the darkened doorway. The figure stepped forward, dressed in a traditional long-sleeved djellaba robe. His wizened face was framed by the stubble of a close-shaved white beard. Then he smiled.

'You must forgive my peregrine falcon; she has a habit of throwing her voice. It confuses people sometimes. But it is amusing.' The old man's eyes twinkled. Rocio couldn't help but laugh. Yet in her heart she knew it was a laugh of relief… relief that it wasn't her who had been chatting with the bird.

'Welcome, travelers, to the caravanserai. I am known here as the Hadji. Please, come in.' The old man pulled back a cloth curtain that covered the doorway and beckoned them to enter.

His face was thin and his eyes were dark and deep set. It was a face that looked as if it had seen many journeys, many sands, and many starry nights.

'First, we speak a little; and then you both wash. Your bodies are the carriers of much sand, and yet your skin is soft like babies!' The Hadji gave a gentle laugh which did not detract from the balance of his lean and calm face.

The three of them sat on cushions in a long room strewn with many colored rugs. The light was shady and cool, and the air was surprisingly fresh. The place was quite bare, containing only the minimal of objects. It seemed to be neither a shrine nor a home.

The Hadji noticed Rocio's inquisitive gaze. 'This is a caravanserai,' he said, looking at Rocio affectionately. 'It is a place for travelers, like you. It is a place of movement. No one stays here for long. Usually only one day and night, sometimes two. The only static things here are the walls, and myself,' he said, pointing a bony finger to his chest.

'A caravanserai, of course. These are the desert inns used for traders traveling the trade routes in the old days.' Rocio's father tried to give her one of his knowledgeable looks.

The Hadji looked across at Luis Rodriguez Rodriguez and the corners of his mouth turned slightly upward. 'That is right, Sidi Moustache.'

Rocio covered her mouth to suppress a giggle.

'Yet the caravanserai,' continued the Hadji, 'was not only for the 'old days' as you say. Journeys never stop. As long as there are people in the world, the journey will always continue to exist. It is said that there are only really two things that truly exist in this world – the leaving upon a journey, and the arrival from a journey. Whatever happens in-between these two things is, well, what we call life. This is the true story of our lives. It is the journey between two ends. And in this, everyone has a story. So, what is yours…something about a lighthouse?'

'Yes. I know it sounds strange, even crazy, but it is something I cannot fully describe in words…' stammered Luis Rodriguez Rodriguez.

The Hadji held up his hand. 'Not all stories demand words. Just provide me with a feeling, and I shall provide you in turn with my feeling. This is the language of men.' The Hadji gave Rocio a look. 'Sorry, the language of the human. You see, even I find words difficult when it comes to true language.'

'It's okay, Hadji,' replied Rocio, 'I'm not listening to the words themselves anyway. I'd like to try to find the feeling, as you say.'

The Hadji nodded. 'And that is why you are the morning dew.' Rocio's heart almost stopped beating in her chest. How had the Hadji known that was the true meaning of her name?

The Hadji smiled. 'There are greater things in this world than words. Now,' he said, turning back to Luis Rodriguez Rodriguez, 'show me the lighthouse you have in your heart.'

Luis Rodriguez Rodriguez closed his eyes and tried to

visualize the dream he had seen all those weeks before. Finally, he spoke. 'It came to me in a dream as a thing of wonder; a great majestic light to guide all travelers along their journeys. A lighthouse that is true does not need to be a lighthouse for the mundane. This lighthouse is not for ships, boats, or donkey smugglers.' Luis Rodriguez Rodriguez gave his daughter a quick smile. His voice was animated now, as a child describing their favorite toys. 'This is a lighthouse for the soul. And the place for the soul is quiet, where only the softest breezes sing their songs in starlight. I was shown that this lighthouse is to be in the desert. And then I awoke with the feeling…no, with the certainty that if I do everything else in this world, yet do not do this one thing, then I will have done nothing. But if I do this one thing, then no matter what else I do in this lifetime I will have done everything.'

Rocio looked at the face of her father. There was something different in it, but she could not say what it was. It was as if something *other* was looking out from his face, and it gave his skin a slightly different glaze.

The Hadji put his hands together as if in prayer and bowed his head. He remained still for several seconds. 'I shall help you, Sidi Moustache. And your daughter too, Morning Dew. Your story is a true one, and it sings in my chest as if it were my own song. Many people have passed through this caravanserai; yet few are those who carry a genuine story in their hearts. Without stories there are no storytellers, and without storytellers there is no world for us to make our journey within. I know the desert place where you need to be, and I will take you there. I am a man of the desert. The sand is my feet, the stars are my eyes, and the desert breeze is my breath.'

The Hadji stood up. 'We have spoken, and we have communicated. And now you must wash and rest, or your smell will scare away the camels.' The Hadji allowed himself the briefest of smiles.

'Thank you,' said Luis Rodriguez Rodriguez.

'No, do not thank me, Sidi Moustache. This is my duty and my honor. It is what *I* do. One should not be thanked for doing what they are here to do. Now you must wash, before the sand becomes your true skin and your land will not welcome you back.'

The Hadji showed Luis Rodriguez Rodriguez and Rocio to one of the bays of the caravanserai. Inside were ample resting quarters, adjoined by a room for bathing.

'Rest,' said the Hadji, 'for tomorrow the caravan shall move on.'

Rocio, now washed and cleaned, gazed up through a cloudless night sky. She felt as if she was looking through a window from this world into another, and stars were the lights that guided the way. She realized then that she knew so little. That there was so much, so much more to do, and to know.

It's okay, Morning Dew, at least we are now at the desert. We've come this far...

She listened quietly to herself as her father slept. Maybe next time, she thought, I will be his mother instead of his daughter. She chuckled quietly to herself.

ELEVEN

Four Camels for Three

*I*t is said a new day waits for no one. Nature has her own rhythms which neither know nor care about the hours, minutes, and seconds of the human clock. In Nature's world everything starts early. Even dawn herself is sometimes late for the desert days. And for those unfamiliar with desert mornings, the early bright glare washes over the ground bringing a luminescence to every grain of sand.

Luis Rodriguez Rodriguez was already awake and outside when Rocio opened the first of her sleepy eyes. This was her preferred method of awaking, with one eye at a time. In this way, if she didn't like the prospect of the coming day, then she could close her one eye before the other one had opened and forced her into wakefulness. It was, however, a neat plan that never seemed to work. Rocio, each day, always found herself getting up eager to know what prospect was in store for her. In the end, no one can know what is to befall a person on any particular day. Rocio, perhaps more than others, was somehow fully aware of this uncertainty.

With both eyes fully open Rocio found her father sitting outside in the morning sun. He was watching the tall, aged Hadji preparing the camels.

'It looks like we're camel riding today.'

'Yes, Papa. Finally, we meet the desert.'

'Are you ready, my little one?'

Luis Rodriguez Rodriguez didn't very often refer to Rocio as his little one, not since she was a young child. She wasn't sure if she still liked this term of endearment. But Papa was her Papa, and she would always be his little one.

She shrugged. 'Ready for what?'

'Yes, exactly.' Her father turned to her and smiled. 'Okay then, let's do it. The desert waits for no one!'

The Hadji was fastening large bags to the last of the four camels. He turned and acknowledged his two guests as they approached.

Rocio looked at the four one-humped camels all lined up together. 'Four camels for three?' she asked.

The Hadji looked at her with a blank expression. A few seconds of silence. 'Three camels for three persons, and one camel for carrying,' he said finally, as if stating the obvious.

'So, these are the dromedaries of the desert,' added Luis Rodriguez Rodriguez as he stroked one of the camels. Several flies were buzzing around annoyingly. 'Mm, authentic,' he whispered quietly.

'Have you had a morning wash?' asked the Hadji.

Both his guests nodded.

'Good. We have only a little water for two days and nights in the desert. After the second night we arrive at Wadi Kabir.'

'Wadi Kabir?' asked Rocio.

The Hadji nodded. 'It is your destination. The oasis of Wadi Kabir is beside the valley where the great river once ran through this desert. It is the perfect place for your lighthouse; both in the desert and in the great valley river, depending on your time frame.'

'Excellent.' Luis Rodriguez Rodriguez slapped his hands together. 'Onwards to Wadi Kabir it is.'

After a light breakfast under the shade of the faded canopy the camel caravan of the desert set out. All four camels were tied together in a line, with the Hadji riding the lead camel, Luis Rodriguez Rodriguez seated on the second camel, Rocio upon the third, and the final fourth camel loaded with supplies. As soon as the camels left the caravanserai the last of the track beneath them disappeared into sand. Both travelers were surprised. They had not known just how close to the desert they had been. In fact, beyond the other side of the caravanserai was nothing but desert and dunes. The caravanserai was the last of the obstacles holding back the encroachment of the sands. Year after year they pushed against the old stone walls. One day the caravanserai too would be no more. One more piece of civilization buried until another age would come again to roll back the tides of sand. And that was how it was, unbeknown to the short lives of busy creatures.

The caravan moved on in silence. Against the grandeur of the desert no words were adequate. As any desert dweller can tell you, anyone without respect for the desert does not last long. Greater forces are at work, ones that humble even the most experienced of travelers.

Riding a one-humped camel may not be the most comfortable form of transport, but it provides ample opportunity for thought and reflection. The camel does not walk fast, although it can run at great speed if requested. But when it walks across the undulating sands it is the most stable of creatures. No one fears a camel falling down in the sands. They were made for the desert horizons.

Luis Rodriguez Rodriguez and his daughter had been brought up in an urban world. They had learnt to adapt to the rigors and constraints of time. Things in their world happened by the ticking hands of a clock. Daily portions of their life were carved out by the dictates of time that nobody truly controlled or even knew. Time was an anonymous figure for them that cast its shadow over their whole lives. Yet time is neither unassailable nor the greatest master – it also has an enemy it does not understand or can defeat. And that enemy is the *now*. Time is either past or future. Contrary to what everyone may tell you, there is no time in the present. Time does not know how to exist in the present. It is an impossible task for it. Instead it slides continually from the future into the past. There are some folks who spend most of their lives trying to hold onto a time in the past; or try to dredge up past time into the present. But time does not belong to the present – only *now* belongs to the present.

Rocio began to quietly understand this as she listened to the desert silence from upon her one-humped camel. There is something magical about camels after all.

The Hadji steered the camels into a grove of palm trees as the sun overhead began to reach its full midday force.

'Here we rest. We eat, talk a little, and then sleep. We move on when the sun is lower,' said the Hadji in a matter-of-fact voice. Soon blankets were spread across the shaded sand and the Hadji started to prepare what turned out to be a delicious lunch of spiced vegetables, a type of pancake, fresh bread and fresh fruit. Luis Rodriguez Rodriguez and Rocio lay back on the blankets as the Hadji boiled some water for tea.

'So, have you always lived at the caravanserai?' asked Luis Rodriguez Rodriguez, wanting to make conversation.

'No, not always. I too had my past, and a life that provided nothing for me. My own destiny took me on a long journey where I became a Hadji. That was before I arrived at the caravanserai.' The older man scratched his thin, bony cheek.

'But if you arrive back the same person, then you have done nothing. And the same things in your mind will haunt you,' he said tapping his head.

'And now you are, what, a camel rider? A guide?'

The Hadji smiled. 'Words again. You use words as if they really had meaning. And if I ride camels, so what? What does that really mean about me?'

Luis Rodriguez Rodriguez shrugged.

The Hadji poured everyone a mug of steaming, sweet tea. 'What I am to you is not important. What I actually do is between I and Thou. I work between the periphery and the center. We all live on the periphery. Our lives of running around here and there; it is nothing but living on the thin edge of a periphery. It is very thin. People do not move much even when they think they do. I speak about movement here.' The Hadji pointed to his chest. 'But there are some, like you, who seek the center. The center you seek is in the desert. I am for you the bridge between these two worlds. I shall take you from the periphery to the center, and then I shall be gone. Along the way we shall talk, tell stories, and share silence. And we shall be at peace with ourselves, or we shall be no one.' The Hadji sipped his tea and his gaze trailed off into the distance.

Rocio looked out across the endless sweep of sand and rolling dunes. To her, it all looked the same. If she were to be alone right now she would have no idea in which direction to go. Yet for a trained desert eye, no two places in the desert are alike. The desert has its personality, its markings and telltale signs. Yet for the untrained eye, it is all one seamless, sameness stretch of sand. And under a shady breeze the desert calls the traveler to easy rest.

They hadn't realized that they had fallen asleep. By the time Luis Rodriguez Rodriguez and Rocio awoke everything was packed away and the camels were ready for the onward journey.

The Hadji nodded his head thoughtfully. 'The sands wish for you to move on. They grant you passage, but you are not of their kind. You sleep too easily upon her and are not wary.' He gave a wry smile, and then waved them onto the camels.

'Why is it always the fourth camel that carries the load? Why don't the camels take turns to carry the things?'

The Hadji rubbed his stubbly chin as he eyed Rocio. 'Yes, for you that is a logical question. Would you have me carry your own bags? I am old, like the three camels that carry us. The fourth camel is the youngest, and so it is her burden. The youth must carry their burden if they wish to be old with honor and experience.'

And the caravan moved on.

The sun was getting low in the sky as the camels marched across the flat sand toward a large dune that rose up as if it were a tsunami of sand stuck in mid motion. The Hadji pointed toward the dune. 'There!'

They made camp at the base of the dune. 'The dune shall protect us from the desert wind,' said the Hadji as he unbuckled the supplies from the fourth camel.

Rocio stared up at the dune and she knew, just knew without any inkling of a doubt that she was going to run up and slide down that mountain of sand. The Hadji laughed, as if knowing her thought.

'Yes, you cannot resist the sand. Go!'

Rocio took off her boots and the sand was warm and soft beneath her bare feet. And then she ran. She ran and she ran, her feet disappearing into the sand, slowing her down. Halfway up the dune she had to stop running. Now she walked, and savored every step she took, loving the feel of the sand beneath her. Finally, she arrived at the top ridge of the dune. She sat down, facing the other side, and breathed in deeply. It was as if she were alone in the world. There was no one and nothing but sand as far as the eye could see. Rocio felt as though she were on top of a world of sand, gazing out over her lonely kingdom. Yes, she felt alone; but not lonely. What Rocio felt was a majestic, noble solitude. She closed her eyes and listened to the desert. She could hear its voice. The Lady of the Sands was whispering, oblivious to the world of men that argued and often raged with itself.

And then Rocio ran down the slope of the dune toward the camp. And she ran, and she ran, faster and faster, being pulled by the slipping of the sands. She felt complete freedom. Free from all the things of the world which had built up around her. All the things telling her this, that, and expecting from her that which were not truly a part of her.

When she arrived at the tent Rocio was exhausted and hungry. This time they ate warm food cooked over the heat of a small gas stove. Inside the tent it was cozy, with rugs and cushions placed upon the floor. When Rocio next looked out of the tent she noticed it was dark.

'Night falls early in the desert,' said the Hadji. 'And light comes early too. In the desert we learn to live by light and darkness.'

'And you just go to sleep when it's dark?'

The Hadji chuckled. 'Ah, Morning Dew, you think we play video games or watch films until the pizza and beer is finished? What, and *then* we go to sleep?! No, we make full use of time by being in synch with it.'

'But you're still wearing a watch,' said Luis Rodriguez Rodriguez, nodding his head at the Hadji's wrist.

'Of course, I have to have something to remind me to laugh!'

The rest of the evening food was eaten in silence. The old man, seemingly with endless energy, cleared the pots away and prepared the hot tea.

'Part of my duty,' he said as he handed out the steaming mugs, 'is to tell a short story each night. This way we pay homage to the desert and the passage from the periphery to the center. And now that we have eaten I will share a tale of time, since it lies in your hands, and upon my wrist,' he said with a gentle smile.

Luis Rodriguez Rodriguez and Rocio leaned back upon their cushions, sipped their tea, and listened to the soft voice of the Hadji.

'Once, a long, long time ago, there was a stream that had its beginnings in faraway mountains. On its journey it passed through a great stretch of countryside until it came to the edge of a vast desert. Since it had crossed every other barrier, it was confident that it could cross the desert. However, no matter how hard it tried, the stream always disappeared in the sand. The stream was convinced that its destiny was to cross this desert, but it could not find a way. It became upset and frightened. Then it heard a whisper from the desert sands.

'The wind crosses the desert and so can the stream.'

The stream listened to the sands and was amazed.

'I have been trying as hard as I can, and anyhow the wind can fly. I am not the wind and I cannot fly,' replied the stream.

'By trying in your accustomed ways, you cannot cross. If you keep doing it, you will either disappear or become a marsh. You must allow the wind to carry you over to your destination.'

'But how can this happen?' asked the stream.

'By allowing yourself to be absorbed into the wind.'

The stream did not like this idea. It had never been absorbed before and was frightened of losing its identity. It thought, *if I lose my identity can I get it back again? Or will I be left formless wandering with the wind forever?*

The desert sands, sensing the stream's fears, spoke. 'This is what the wind does. It takes up water as vapor and carries it over the desert, and then lets it fall again. By falling as rain, the water again becomes a stream.'

'How can I be sure of that?' asked the water.

'It is so, and if you do not believe it, you cannot become more than a marsh; and even that could take many, many years, and that is certainly not the same as a stream.'

'But can I not remain the same stream as I am today?'

'You cannot in either case remain so,' whispered the sands. 'Your essential part is carried away and forms a stream again. Even though you are called a stream, and feel a stream, you do not know which part of you is the essential one.'

On hearing this, vague echoes began to awaken for the stream – dim memories of being held by the wind. It thought, *maybe this is the real thing to do, though not the obvious thing to do.*

So, with a leap of faith the stream let go and began to rise as vapor into the welcoming arms of the wind. It was lifted gently upwards and taken over the desert to finally fall as soft rain as it reached the roof of a mountain, many miles away. Soon it became a stream once again. The stream was able to remember the details of the experience and reflected - *now I have learned my true identity.*

The desert sands whispered: 'We know because we see it happen every day; and because the sands extend from the riverside all the way to the mountains.'

The Hadji nodded his head slowly. 'And that is why it is said that the way of the journey of the stream of life is written in the sands.' The old man looked across at Rocio and her father. 'The stories of the desert are *real* stories. And they affect all those who know how to listen.'

The Hadji got up and walked toward the entrance of the tent. 'Sleep well, Sidi Moustache and Morning Dew. Tomorrow morning the caravan moves on. We shall move with the rising of the sun. Remember, we are in a different time here.'

'Where are you going?' asked Luis Rodriguez Rodriguez.

The Hadji smiled. 'I am a man of the desert. I sleep under the stars.' And then he stepped out of the tent and into the darkness of the desert.

Rocio washed her hands and face with water from a bottle. Her father was helping the Hadji pack away the tent and utensils. It was then she noticed that the fourth camel, the younger one, had one of its legs tied backward underneath itself. It was standing on three legs. Surely, thought Rocio, that is not the way for a caravan to treat its camels. She made a mental note to bring this up later with the Hadji. She glanced over at her father who had his now familiar blue scarf wrapped around his head. She thought his face looked more rugged, and less clean shaven. Luis Rodriguez Rodriguez of Arabia, she mused with a grin.

The three of them mounted the camels. Just before the Hadji had mounted his lead camel he untied the leg of the fourth. And then they were on their way again.

The desert had shared some of its own eerie calm. During the night Rocio had listened to the silence and recognized it as a different sound than the silence she had known back home. This silence was more profound and sincere. It was a silence of honesty, of truthfulness, and of simplicity. Rocio had slept soundly, dreaming of things only the deepest part of the mind ever remembers.

Luis Rodriguez Rodriguez also felt something special about the desert. It was as if it understood him. It seemed to know about his quest. Perhaps everyone in the desert either has a quest or finds a quest, he thought. Otherwise, one would become lost. The desert is not an easy place for a placeless person. If you enter the desert half lost, you will soon become completely lost. Yet if a person enters half full, then the desert may replenish them further.

There was no sense of the passing time. The dunes repeated themselves over and over. How was it, wondered Rocio, that the Hadji knew in which direction to take them? And yet, as the sun once again rose high towards its zenith, they approached a gathering of palm trees. As if on perfect cue they stopped for their rest.

Rocio had her question falling off the tip of her tongue. As they sat down on the rug to eat the Hadji nodded over to her.

'You may ask now.'

'Ask what?' Rocio tried to look casual.

The Hadji just smiled.

'Okay then. Why did you tie up that camel's leg? Was it as a punishment?'

The Hadji shook his head. 'Punishment is a sad, human game. That young camel is, like all youngsters, an inquisitive spirit. She likes to wander off, especially at night under the stars when the rest of us are in our dream worlds. She must learn that to become an adult there are many caravans to assist across the desert.' The Hadji opened his hands in a gesture. 'So, I tied her leg to stop her from leaving us with only three camels for three people. As they say in the desert - trust in fate but tie your camels first.' The Hadji laughed, and his old, thin face lit up.

Rocio thought there was something familiar about that phrase. She felt she had heard something similar before, but for now she just couldn't quite place it.

'Do you know why a camel never falls down in the desert sands?' asked the Hadji. He looked at both Luis Rodriguez Rodriguez and Rocio. They shook their heads.

'Because of its wide, flat feet?' Rocio knew it was a wild guess.

'That may help, but it is not the true reason. It is because, like most things in this world, it is a question of perspective. The camel chooses to always look ahead rather than down at its feet. That way, it sees what is coming from far away and is prepared for it when it arrives. The camel doesn't need to look down. It knows what is beneath its feet because it has seen it coming. That is the difference and is perhaps why people are always falling down.'

Luis Rodriguez Rodriguez laughed out loud. Rocio looked at him in surprise. She wasn't used to hearing such spontaneous laughter coming from her father.

The Hadji grinned. 'Sidi Moustache liked that one!'

After their midday rest the caravan again moved on as if following the arc of the descending sun. Everything in the desert was attuned to the movement of the sun and the stars. As the sun slipped into its nighttime retreat it was time for the canopy of stars to twinkle their faraway lights over the desert sands.

The caravan finally came to a halt in a dip between two sand dunes. The dusky sky was mellow, and a calm hue enveloped everything. Already several stars could be seen poking through overhead. The Hadji came over to where Rocio was standing, her head thrown back as she gazed at the stars. He pointed into the sky with his thin finger.

'There she goes,' he said in a soft voice.

'Where who goes?' asked Rocio.

'There goes *our* star – we follow her just as she follows her destiny. That star there is the one you know as Aldebaran. We know her as al-dabaran, and her name means 'the Follower.' We follow her just as we all follow one's true destiny.' The Hadji gently took Rocio's hand and pointed her finger towards the star Aldebaran. 'Remember her,' he said quietly.

The desert night fell over the tent and gave the travelers a sense of protected seclusion. Again, the Hadji prepared some delicious food seemingly out of nowhere. The desert ways were indeed both subtle and surprising.

'And now,' said the Hadji as they had finished eating, 'I shall tell you another tale that belongs to us.'

Luis Rodriguez Rodriguez and Rocio made themselves comfortable upon the cushions.

'A desert legend tells of two friends who were traveling through the desert and at one point they fell into disagreement about their journey. Suddenly one of the friends slapped the other one across the face. The friend who had been slapped said nothing, only wrote in the sand: 'Today my best friend slapped me in the face.' Both friends continued on their journey and eventually they arrived at an oasis where there were pools to refresh themselves. The friend who had been slapped jumped into a large pool, yet soon found himself starting to drown. The other friend immediately jumped in after him and saved him. After recovering, the first man took his sharp knife and etched upon a stone: 'Today my best friend saved my life.'

Intrigued, the friend asked: 'Why is it that after I hurt you, you wrote in the sand and now after saving you, you write on a stone?' Smiling, the other friend replied: 'When a good friend offends us, we write in the sand where the wind of forgetfulness and forgiveness will be responsible for clearing it off. Yet when something great happens to us, we burn it into stone in memory of the heart where no wind in the world can erase it."

The Hadji got up and went outside to sleep.

Rocio stood alone under the desert sky. She sensed worlds upon worlds moving above her, shifting through their own times and rhythms. She breathed in deeply. She thought she could taste the sweetness of the cosmos. She looked up into the heart of her star. 'Who is following who?' she whispered. A plume of light streaked across the starry sky and burnt up into a sprinkle of nothingness. A distant light had shone briefly for anyone who had eyes and hearts to see.

Tomorrow, the caravan would move on.

The Oasis

TWELVE

Wadi Kabir

The Hadji untied the leg of the fourth camel, and Rocio looked on saying nothing. Today the caravan would be moving out of the desert dunes and into an oasis. It would still be the desert, but in the oasis there would be people and life, instead of the silence of the sands. During breakfast the Hadji announced that today they would reach the oasis of Wadi Kabir. And maybe, if their stars were guiding them, they would find it a suitable place for their lighthouse.

They packed up their belongings and stores and mounted the waiting camels. Rocio looked at her father; she knew that neither of them had any idea how the next part of their journey would go. Building a lighthouse is not only about bricks and mortar and putting materials together. It is also about the human materials, and the place. Would the people at Wadi Kabir be the right people to accept a lighthouse to be built amongst them - in the very place where they lived? Would *this* oasis be the right place for her father's dream? People and place were just as important as the actual construction. How could her father know all these things? Or did he even have to know? Rocio shook her head; there were too many thoughts.

Luis Rodriguez Rodriguez tied the blue scarf tighter around his head and gave his daughter a wink. Whatever lay in store for them, he was ready. An architect is not a true architect if he cannot deal with plans within plans, or even unknown plans. Or at least so thought Luis Rodriguez Rodriguez. It was his way of self-reassurance amidst a whole lot of uncertainties and unknowns. In fact, beyond building a sixty-two-foot lighthouse in the desert, Luis Rodriguez Rodriguez had few other plans. The worst thing that could happen is that I lose myself, he thought. Then he glanced behind him at his daughter Rocio on the third camel. No, there are worse things, he mumbled under his breath. He knew his daughter had trust in him – and love – and neither of these he could afford to lose.

After some time upon the sandy trek the wind began to rise. The camels felt if first. They lifted up their heads and sniffed the air; then they pulled back their gums and showed their teeth. As the wind rose it began to shift the sands. The whole floor of the desert began moving as if it were a flowing sea of silicon droplets. The Hadji raised his hand and the caravan halted. He indicated for every rider to dismount. The Hadji took a length of rope from a sack and tied back one of the legs of the fourth camel. The fourth camel instinctively sat down, and the other three camels followed.

'All the camels are tied together so they won't be going far,' said the Hadji. 'But just in case...'

'I know,' said Rocio. 'Trust in fate but tie your camels first.'

The Hadji grinned. He then took another length of rope from the sack and beckoned for the others to sit down with him against the camels.

'There is a sand storm coming, and humans are less trustworthy than camels. Here, take this rope and tie it around both of your waists before passing it to me.'

Luis Rodriguez Rodriguez tied the rope around his waist and then passed it to his daughter who did likewise. Then Rocio passed the rope to the Hadji. The wind had risen dramatically in only the last few minutes. Where once the horizon had been far and clear, now it was a blurry haze of sand particles dancing dangerously. The quiet whispers of the desert had been replaced by the howls of lesser djinns.

'This rope will stop us from losing each other,' shouted the Hadji over the rising noise. 'But I cannot guarantee it won't stop you from losing yourself!' The Hadji laughed.

'Humor at a time like this!' shouted back Rocio.

'Humor will protect you more than fear,' replied the Hadji.

Then they all bent their heads and shielded their eyes. The three of them - Luis Rodriguez Rodriguez, Rocio, and the Hadji – were bound together by rope; and by circumstances.

The sand djinns were having a wild time creating a feral desert storm. Luis Rodriguez Rodriguez closed his eyes tight and imagined himself constructing the lighthouse. He wanted to play it out in his mind so that when he came to build it he would not have to start from scratch. The whole construction would have already been mapped out in his inner vision. He knew he wanted the base to be firm and wide like a circular oracle.

Rocio felt alone. Although surrounded by two men and four camels, and endless desert djinns, she suddenly felt deeply alone. And when you feel alone, that's when the archetypal questions arise in the back of the mind. *Who am I? No, really, who am I? And what am I doing here? No, not in the desert...in this life? Why am I here, and what do I need to do?* Dangerous questions for anyone at the best of times. But when these become the principal thoughts in your head in the middle of a sand storm in some desert somewhere...well, then there's little escape. The only escape was...

...a hand. Luis Rodriguez Rodriguez had reached over for his daughter's hand. He placed her thin, delicate fingers within his, and squeezed. Yes, that was better. Then Rocio did something she hadn't expected she would. She reached out with her other hand and felt for the hand of the Hadji. His worn yet warm fingers connected with hers and squeezed back. There, that was it – the storm wasn't so bad after all. She hadn't lost herself. She had found something important.

154

And time, sand, wind, and djinn all seemed to meld into one uncategorizable thing. And without a name, an identity, it had no real power, and soon began to dissipate into its separate parts until everything that had come together now fell apart.

The storm passed. Eyes opened, and hands unclasped.

They untied the rope and shook the sand from their clothes. They looked about them and saw another desert. A desert similar to the earlier one, just somehow different as if it all had been shaken by some giant hand. Rocio caught the eye of the Hadji and immediately tried to look away.

'I understand, Morning Dew,' he said quietly so her father could not hear. 'In the land of sand, the human hand is king.' And then he untied the rope from the leg of the fourth camel.

And the caravan moved on.

It was late afternoon when the camels and their riders entered the oasis of Wadi Kabir. A splattering of mud-brick buildings were interspersed between palm trees, tracks, and what appeared to be some well-kept irrigated land with plants. The four camels strode down the main track of the settlement until they came to an open area. Here they dismounted and the Hadji took the camels to a drinking trough by a side wall. 'Come. We make our presence known.' The Hadji waved for

Luis Rodriguez Rodriguez and Rocio to follow. As they passed an open doorway the Hadji suddenly said 'Wait!' and jumped in. Within a few moments he returned with some things in his hand. 'Here, take these.'

The Hadji handed Luis Rodriguez Rodriguez and Rocio a bottle of water and a couple of muesli-nut bars.

'Bottled water – here!' Luis Rodriguez Rodriguez seemed surprised.

The Hadji shrugged. 'Of course, this isn't the stone age. We get your western water delivered here.' Then he sighed. 'But first it comes from Fiji.'

Luis Rodriguez Rodriguez handed him back the bottled water. 'No thanks. What comes from Fiji should stay in Fiji.'

At the end of the settlement of Wadi Kabir was a larger mud brick house that had a garden of neat rows filled with green leafy vegetables. The Hadji motioned for his fellow travelers to wait whilst he went inside.

'First, I must pay my respects to the Village Elder. Then you both can come.' The Hadji disappeared through a doorway.

Luis Rodriguez Rodriguez looked at Rocio with a questioning look.

Rocio looked around. 'Finally, at the oasis. Do you think this will be the place?'

Her father shrugged. 'I really can't say just yet. Maybe I need a sign or something.' He then scratched his chin in a way that Rocio recognized was one of his 'not so sure' gestures.

Then they heard a whistle and looked around to see the Hadji waving for them to come over.

They entered the cool interior of the mud-brick house and followed the Hadji into a main room. At first they couldn't make out anyone, and then they saw a figure seated in a large chair in the corner.

'Come here,' said a female voice. 'Don't be afraid of little ol' Nur. She can be a beast to her enemies but my dear friend Hadji here tells me you are of our ilk.'

Luis Rodriguez Rodriguez and Rocio stepped further into the room and saw a thin, frail-looking old lady beckoning them over with her bony finger.

'So, this is Sidi Moustache and his daughter Morning Dew, eh?' Luis Rodriguez Rodriguez cleared his throat. 'Actually, my name is Luis Rodriguez Rodriguez, and this here is my daughter, Rocio.'

The old lady let out a cackle. 'Sure it is, sure it is. Look, it don't matter who in the world calls you whatever. You are who you are, and that's who I'm looking at right now. Come closer, I don't bite.'

Soon Luis Rodriguez Rodriguez and Rocio were right next to the old lady. Her body may have looked frail, yet her eyes were as sharp as a falcon's beak and as deep as a desert well. She had long black-greying hair falling past her shoulders, which she didn't seem to care about.

'Yes, yes,' she muttered under her breath. 'So these are they.'

'Sorry?'

'Mister, what took you so long?' asked the old lady, completely ignoring his earlier remark.

'So long – for what?'

'Smart cookie.' Her tone was on the sarcastic side.

'We had to learn how to arrive,' interjected Rocio.

The old lady turned and gave her a penetrating gaze. 'She's definitely got it.' She then leaned forward towards the both of them. 'So, whys you here then?'

Luis Rodriguez Rodriguez coughed. 'Well, all I know is that I have to do this. If I do everything else in this world, yet do not do this one thing, then I will have done nothing...'

'But,' interrupted the old lady, 'if I do this one thing, then no matter what else I do in this lifetime I will have done everything.'

Luis Rodriguez Rodriguez breathed a sigh of relief. Finally, he thought.

'As I said, I'm Nur, and I'm the light around here. If anyone wants to build a bigger light, then they sure need to speak with me first. You're fortunate that Hadji here has enabled you to enter without a struggle. The rest is in your hands.' Nur opened her hands and offered them, palm upwards, to her guests. 'We've been waiting for a lighthouse to arrive. So, if that isn't a big enough sign for you then all the billboards of New York aren't going to help you!' Nur laughed and nodded in Luis Rodriguez Rodriguez's direction. 'So, now then, where are you going to build this most wondrous lighthouse of strange delights?'

Luis Rodriguez Rodriguez scratched his chin. 'Over there.'

The Hadji accompanied his traveling guests through the settlement of Wadi Kabir and stopped in front of a medium-sized building.

'Nur has given you residence here. She calls it her *Sand BnB*,' he said with a smile. 'But really it's the old library. You won't have the place to yourselves, but I'm sure you'll be just fine.'

'And you, Hadji – where are you going to stay?' Rocio looked at the old man with a fondness. He had taken them safely through the desert, with four camels for three persons, and delivered them at their destination.

'Me? Well, the Hadji here will be heading back to his caravanserai. You never know how many lost tourists are going to turn up looking like Lawrence of Arabia.' The wizened old face broke into a cheery smile.

'You're going back already?' Rocio's face fell.

'Sure am. Over in that direction it's only one day's travel.'

Rocio looked puzzled. 'Only one day?'

'Sure thing. Going back always takes less time than arriving. Remember that, Morning Dew – arriving always takes longer than going back.' The Hadji then turned to Luis Rodriguez Rodriguez. 'And you, Sidi Moustache, look after your girl.

Your lighthouse is going to need a heart too.'

Luis Rodriguez Rodriguez nodded. 'Is there anything we can give you for your kindness and your trouble?'

The old man shook his head. 'You both have been no trouble. You're the kind of travelers a caravanserai is waiting for. The rest is a distraction.' Then he looked squarely into the eyes of Luis Rodriguez Rodriguez. 'Just give us all light.'

Four camels with one person left the oasis of Wadi Kabir and followed its star into the desert sands.

Rocio smiled despite a tinge of sadness within her. 'Well, I guess it's no more Sidi Moustache for you, Papa.'

'That's right, Morning Dew.' And he unwound his blue scarf.

They seemed to be the only occupants of their *Sand BnB*. And as for it being an old library; well, there were no books to be seen at all. It was a sparsely arranged yet comfortable dwelling. Rocio, for her part, was glad to be in a place with a bed again. After several days on a camel's back she had realized that her body was the soft European type, which meant it didn't adapt too well to desert camels. And she also needed a real wash. It wasn't long before Rocio was fast asleep upon her bed and drifting into the ethers where dreams dwell and devas whisper their delightful ideas.

Luis Rodriguez Rodriguez was sat on a tattered bench outside, looking up at the clear night sky. Soon he would be introducing his own luminous spire into the cloister of starlight. It would be an act of giving, of service. That he was sure of. The rest would be hard work.

Before he knew it, a figure came and sat down on the bench beside him. It was Nur, the Elder of Wadi Kabir.

'I thought I would come to give you some credibility here.' She sniffed. 'You're still a stranger, an outsider. People here will take the both of you for lost tourists and will try to sell you everything. But when people will say that Nur sat with them, then they'll know you're neither tourists nor gullible customers. They'll know you've got my blessing. It's important around here. And I'll spread the word about your special lighthouse. Don't you worry. Everyone has their tasks to do.'

'Thank you, Nur.'

The old lady casually waved her hand.

'And…' Luis Rodriguez Rodriguez hesitated. 'May I ask if you were born here, in Wadi Kabir.'

'You may.'

Then after a short silence. 'Nur, were you born here in Wadi Kabir?'

'No, I wasn't.'

Another silence. Nur turned to Luis Rodriguez Rodriguez. 'Didn't anyone ever teach you not to ask yes or no questions? Fundamental stuff.'

Luis Rodriguez Rodriguez didn't know what to say.

'Look,' continued Nur, 'you may not be very good at asking questions, so you should learn to listen more. Listening more and speaking less is a good thing anyway. If you know *how* to listen, you can learn the great secrets. This lighthouse of yours came about through listening. You may call it a dream; but dreams are just places where you go at night to listen. I have been in the desert all my life, and I didn't need to go anywhere to learn things of value. Not for me. But everyone has their own way. Here I have learnt something very valuable. You could call it a great secret, if such words suited you. I will call it nothing, for my steps to achieve it were greater than the secret itself. And my steps I cannot give to you. What's more, I can tell you nothing of it, for it would be useless to do so. In fact, the secret itself may disappear by the very words used to describe it. Of this nothing more can be said.'

Nur got up from the bench and waved to a passerby.
'Look, you're getting credibility now,' she said to Luis Rodriguez Rodriguez. 'But the rest is up to you. You've got some hard work ahead of you, and not everyone will be convinced about what you're doing. But at least I'm looking forward to seeing this lighthouse.' The old lady walked away as if she had the feet of a fifteen-year-old.

THIRTEEN

The Old Library

*I*n the morning Rocio explored the Old Library to see whether there were any books lying around. After carefully checking, she discovered that one of the rooms was occupied; though that person, whoever he was, was absent.

'Papa, there is another person living in this house, but he's not here. I think it's a man.'

'Why do you say that?'

'The room is a mess. There are nuts, or rather nut shells, all over the floor.'

'Intriguing…'

'Are you listening, Papa?'

'With one ear, yes.'

Rocio gave him a daughter's look. 'And with the other ear?'

'With my other ear I'm listening for a direction. I need to know where to build the lighthouse. It can't just go anywhere.

It has to be in its place. Everything has its place. Things that are not in their place are just…well…just not right.'

'If you're going to do something then you might as well do it right.'

Luis Rodriguez Rodriguez shot his daughter a look.

'That's right,' said Rocio, 'you taught me that as a young girl.'

Her father smiled. Indeed, everything needed to be in its right place. And that included a daughter by his side.

'Come on, Papa, let's go for a stroll.'

Luis Rodriguez Rodriguez and Rocio went walking through the oasis of Wadi Kabir, which was a combination of mud-brick dwellings surrounded by groups of palm trees. Interspersed were plots of irrigated land. In-between ran dust tracks, and…and donkeys!

'Do you think Nash knows about this place?'

'Knows about it?!' Luis Rodriguez Rodriguez laughed. 'I'm sure he's the one who sold them all their donkeys!'

'An oasis full of donkeys,' muttered Rocio under her breath. 'You trickster, Nash, you knew all along!'

'What was that, dear?'

'Nothing, Papa. I was just thinking kindly of our rogue friend, Nash. Do you think that a person's destination is already mapped out? I mean, already known before they get there?'

'In a way I think it must be. Otherwise, how would we know it even existed? How can we be pulled toward a final destination if it's not there in the first place?'

'So, if the destination already exists then why don't we just go there directly and cut out the middle part?'

Luis Rodriguez Rodriguez laughed again. 'I guess you can't go there without a map. And that's why we need a journey, it's the map. Remember what the Hadji said - arriving always takes longer than going back.'

As they walked through Wadi Kabir passers-by would turn their heads and look at them. A few waved and smiled whilst the rest seemed curious. The oasis had strangers in its midst, walking upon her sandy, hard, mud earth. Luis Rodriguez Rodriguez had no doubt that Nur had been true to her word when she said she had given them credibility. Yet credibility also has to be earned and is not a title one receives lightly. In a small place such as Wadi Kabir, news travels faster than a speeding camel. And within the blink of an eye everybody knows your business. Now this wouldn't work so well in the city – blinks of eyes, speeding camels, and everyone knowing your business are not the kind of things that sit well in a crowded city. But in small communities, such as an oasis, these connections and knowings are essential. No man is an island, or so it is said. And in Wadi Kabir no person lives with their front door locked. That is because everyone sees and knows everyone else. Naturally, they are cautious when strangers turn up on their doorstep.

The folk of Wadi Kabir seemed to be busy doing relatively nothing. Or rather, they appeared to be doing nothing whilst busying themselves with matters. The interior sandy lanes were dotted with the older inhabitants sitting around in their djellabas eyeing the floating particles of dust as they mingled with the air. Rocio felt that there was something both familiar and yet strange about the place, as if it *could* be in a dream and yet was so very dusty and real at the same time. There was a line somewhere that was blurred, and neither side knew how to straighten it. Rocio noticed two old men sitting on faded, plastic chairs. One of the men smiled and beckoned her over.

'Look, Papa, they want to say something.' Rocio nudged her father and nodded at the men. They both crossed over and approached the old men with a greeting.

The first old man continued smiling. Rocio noticed that the old man's mouth possessed few teeth when he laughed. Finally, the man lifted a bony finger and began to speak. 'God provides the food, men provide the cooks.'

The old man's companion had sat all this time with a stony expression on his face in stark contrast. Now he leaned forward and as if adding to the previous comment said, 'But if you insist on buying poor food, you must be prepared to dislike it at the serving.'

There was a pause where some of the dust particles gathered. 'Thank you, gentlemen' replied Luis Rodriguez Rodriguez.

'Instructive cooking metaphors,' said Rocio as they were further down the road.

'Yes. Meaning in food,' agreed her father.

Soon they passed a series of single-story mud brick buildings with voices mingling inside. Rocio stopped and went over to one of the low square openings that served as a window. A cool raft of air blew into her face. She closed her eyes and enjoyed the chill. And then she saw all the other faces. A classroom of school children had turned to look at her. A little girl laughed, and then the whole room burst out into laughter. Rocio instinctively pulled her head away.

'What's that?'

Rocio turned to her father and started to laugh nervously. 'I think I've just become a classroom joke.'

Luis Rodriguez Rodriguez smiled. 'We both might be a joke here for a little while longer.'

They continued walking, and almost without deciding it they ended up following a lone donkey down a dusty track. Now, in most cases this would seem a slightly odd thing to do. In the normal run of things, it should be donkeys that follow people. But Luis Rodriguez Rodriguez and Rocio had come to learn at least the part about not getting pulled into the 'normal run of things.' So, if you're going to get anywhere that is truly meaningful then you need to follow the signs – whether they are donkeys, dates, or the blind. And right now, following one of Nash's possible donkeys seemed like a fine idea. Oh, and that's another thing – always be wary of following 'fine ideas' unless you're sure that doing anything else would be, well, even crazier.

The donkey led the two intrepid followers out of the oasis and into a flat piece of dusty, hard land. The donkey kept walking, heading to nowhere that was visible, until it suddenly stopped. It lowered its head and began to nibble. Luis Rodriguez Rodriguez and Rocio reached where the donkey was and saw that it was chewing on the one shrub that had grown out of a crack in the mud floor. When it had finished chewing it stepped over to Rocio and nuzzled against her. Rocio stroked its long nose and looked into the donkey's eyes.

'What do you see?' Luis Rodriguez Rodriguez was suddenly intrigued.

'Papa, it's just a donkey. Please, don't overdo this one.'

'A donkey to you is an omen to me.' Luis Rodriguez Rodriguez looked around him at the open space in all directions. And the ground was flat and hard. It was perfect. He stepped onto the spot where the shrub had once been.

'We've found the spot! I'm not leaving this spot until we mark it. Quick, go back to the Old Library and get something to mark this spot.' Luis Rodriguez Rodriguez unrolled the now tatty blue scarf that had been in his pocket and placed it over his head. 'I'm staying here, Rocio, until you come back to mark the spot. So you better get going before I melt!'

'Papa!!' Rocio turned around and marched away quickly.

The donkey slowly plodded behind.

Back at the Old Library Rocio hurried through the front
entrance and ran into him. That is, she smacked into his bulky
frame and something fell down. But it wasn't her. A huge
hand picked up a squawking grey thing and placed it on the
man's large back.

'Hey, lass, what you running into things for?'

Rocio stepped back and took a few deep breaths. 'Sorry, I,
well, I just…sorry – who are you?'

The large man offered his hand. 'They call me Kenzie. I
dropped my Mc before I got here.'

Rocio took the man's large hand which completely engulfed
her own. 'Hi, I'm Rocio. Sorry, where did you drop your Mac?
Did you lose your computer? I don't understand.'

The man laughed. He had a large face covered with a bushy,
dark beard and looked to be somewhere in his fifties. He had
a tight-cropped head of curly dark hair and a sun-tanned,
ruddy face. Fearsome yet jovial was Rocio's first thought.

'So, you must be the lighthouse builder's daughter? Welcome
to my humble abode.'

Rocio looked surprised. And then she clicked. 'Ah, so you're
staying here too?'

'Oh yes, lass, this is my place; has been for years. They put you
with me as I'm not from round here either.'

'Sorry, but I thought this place was the Old Library.'

'It is.' A huge grin burst across Kenzie's face. 'That's what they sometimes call me – the Old Library. Hah!' And then the grey thing squawked. 'Ah, and this is Monkey.' A pair of rounded brown eyes in a fluffy grey face peered over from Kenzie's shoulder.

'You've got a monkey on your back?' Rocio asked matter-of-factly. Or rather, it was more a statement than a question.

Kenzie nodded. 'Yeah, I got a monkey on my back.'

The both of them looked at each other. It was hard for anyone to follow a statement like that. Then Rocio suddenly remembered.

'Papa!'

After quickly explaining what she needed Rocio left the Old Library with Kenzie in tow. They made their way through the oasis and out into the open plain where Luis Rodriguez Rodriguez was still standing, determined as ever not to lose his precious spot. Kenzie dropped the large rock he had been hauling.

'There you go. That rock will mark the spot for you.'

Luis Rodriguez Rodriguez looked at the big man Kenzie.

'You've got a monkey on your back.'

'Aye, and you've got a scruffy blue scarf on your head, but I won't hold it against you.'

At least they had marked the spot.

The next thing was for Luis Rodriguez Rodriguez to become the architect he always was. Back at the house the three of them sat down and rested. Kenzie explained that once he had been a librarian, but that he preferred to read books rather than shelve them. So one day he decided to take a bunch of books and became a sailor. He had worked on various trade ships until he decided to finally come ashore for the last time. Just before embarking at the North African port he found monkey as a stowaway.

'Maybe he escaped from the Rock of Monkeys,' added Rocio enthusiastically. 'Remember, Papa, what Nash said – its monkeys all the way down, and many a country has tried to conquer it but the monkeys always fight them off.'

'That's right, Rocio. It's monkeys all the way down.'

'All the way down,' repeated Kenzie.

'And so why the Old Library?'

'Because I am the library. I have all the books inside of me… and I'm no longer as young as I once was. That was Nur who named me the Old Library. I think it was her sense of humor, the crazy old sorceress. She sure is a blast, that woman!'

Kenzie cracked several nuts together in the palm of one of his hands. He then reached up and the grey hand of Monkey snatched the nuts from his hand.

'Aye, Monkey – that's a good monkey.'

Rocio thought the whole scene seemed normal now. Her

father seemed nonplussed as he sat there adding the finishing touches to the lighthouse in his mind. And he had great plans for Kenzie. He would come in very useful. Indeed, Nur was a crafty sorceress.

Rocio wondered how many books Kenzie, the Old Library, had inside of him. He had said that he still carries the books around with him but that he prefers to live life now rather than to read. 'If I live life then I can see if my experiences match with any of the stories in my books,' he had said.

'And do they? Rocio had asked.

'Not much of the time. Books I think have an odd perspective on life, as if looking through a shard of colored glass. I've come to call it the Splinter Perspective.'

And now Kenzie was getting a new experience to add to his repertoire. It was very probable that Kenzie had never read a book about an ex-librarian who adopted a monkey and later became foreman for a project to construct a lighthouse in the desert. If such a book had never been written, then it surely deserved to be. Maybe that would be Kenzie's next experience – to write his own story to carry around in his head. But then experience and story would become oddly entangled; and who would know where fantasy stopped and reality started?

Later that night the three of them - Luis Rodriguez Rodriguez, Rocio, and Kenzie – were sitting on the bench outside, each drifting into their own thoughts as the stars glittered overhead. Monkey took a cracked nut from Kenzie's hand and chewed. The deep eyes in his furry grey head were observing the world and making their own splintered perspectives.

'So, you know enough locals then?' asked Luis Rodriguez Rodriguez.

Kenzie nodded. 'Aye. That won't be a problem. We've got enough physical hands-on power here.'

'Will they do it – build a lighthouse?'

'If there's enough fortunate factors involved. Things are never either singular or simple here. There needs to be a mix of at least three factors.'

'And what three do you think we need?'

'We need them to have sufficient curiosity and that they like you.'

'Well, that's two, if I'm counting correctly.'

'Ah yes, and the third is that if Nur tells them to!'

'And will she?'

'Have you asked her?'

Luis Rodriguez Rodriguez scratched his chin. 'Good point.'

Rocio stood up and stretched her legs. 'I'm going for a little walk.'

A real desert oasis is not always like the type of oasis that many books would have you believe. Adventure books are filled with images of lush havens of spouting water, verdant trees and greenery, and plentiful fruits that quench the thirst and hunger of needy travelers. A modern oasis, on the other hand, is a settlement that has arisen around a source of water, whether it's a pretty sight or not.

Rocio looked up at the mud-brick dwelling and called out through the open door. She waited, and when there was no answer she called again.

'What's all the hollering?' said a voice.

Rocio turned around to see Nur standing a few feet behind her, near one of the trees.

'Oh, I thought you were inside?'

'No, my dear – you *assumed* I was inside. It's not quite the same thing.' Nur smiled. 'Come, walk with me – before you wake up the sleeping desert with your howling.'

Rocio followed Nur as she led the way down one of the tracks of Wadi Kabir.

'This oasis is a fertile place,' said Nur after several minutes of silence.

Rocio nodded. 'Yes, a place of water in the desert.'

'That is one type of oasis – one meaning of fertility. There are others.'

They stopped by a domed building. Nur walked around the

building slowly with Rocio walking close behind. Through the moonlight Rocio could see that the outer mud walls of the domed building were carved with shapes – a mosaic of geometric patterns.

'Fertility also applies to the mind and heart. If one is fertile inside, then there is movement. There is change, progress. If the well of the human heart is dry then everything else dries up, and there is little or no momentum. Fertility is an essential ingredient for the human spirit. Everyone you have met on your way here was, in one way or another, on the move. No-one was static. That is the nature of the caravan of life. It moves on – it *must* move on. There are only resting places. Places where those of the caravan can recuperate.

'The caravanserai?' asked Rocio.

Nur nodded. Her aged head moved slowly yet gracefully. 'The caravanserai is one such place. Yet it offers physical rest only. Sometimes there is a need for something deeper.' Nur walked to the edge of the wall and placed her hand upon a large corner stone. 'Here,' she said. 'This will tell you.'

Rocio stepped forward and looked. She could just make out the shape of a palm tree sculptured into the brickwork.

'What does a palm tree symbolize – an oasis?'

'A special type of oasis. In this world there are always people on the move – people with a special function. They are ceaselessly moving in the world. They are what some of us would call *invisible people*. They are not truly invisible but are physical just like you and me. Yet they are invisible because all but a very

175

few people know of what they do.' Nur paused to look at Rocio. Rocio stayed silent. She didn't know what to say so she thought it best to say nothing. 'These invisibles,' continued Nur, 'visit communities throughout the world. And by doing so, they help spread a certain type of energy. It is a special energy that is needed in the world. Of this nothing more can be said. Yet at times these people need rest too. And they need to rest in fertile places, where they can be replenished. Such places that have this type of replenishing energy are marked by the sign of the palm tree. Our Friends come here to rest before they are to move on again and continue with their work.'

'Like a place of healing – a natural spring?'

Nur took Rocio by the arm. 'Yes, dear – something like that. They are places of special healing.'

Nur took Rocio and walked with her down the track that led away from Wadi Kabir. Soon they were looking out into the clear distance. Nur pointed with her bony finger.

'And out there will be your lighthouse.' Nur poked Rocio in the arm. 'When you bring a special light to a special place, then you get a little special magic. What say you, daughter of Sidi Moustache?'

Rocio laughed. 'Yes, there is going to be magic. A special magic.'

'That's right. Things like this don't occur for no reason. Individuals, communities, and nations – we all have our time and our reasons. And when time and reason are aligned, then the opportunity should not be missed. Missed opportunities and words spoken in haste are two arrows that pierce us. Now – what was your question?'

Rocío hesitated. 'Question?'

'Yes, dear child – the reason why you came visiting this evening. I'm sure it wasn't only for my charm.'

'Oh, yes…that. Well, I just wanted to ask if you and your community would help us to build the lighthouse. We need physical help and resources too.'

Nur threw up her hands. 'Oh – you're all so European! Look, you wouldn't be here if we weren't going to help you. My girl, you wouldn't have made it an inch of your way here without help. Stop looking at your feet and start to feel the path.'

Nur turned around and quickly began walking away.

'There'll be a song in it for you!' she called back.

'What?' But it was too late. Nur had already slipped away.

It was then that Rocio spotted the donkey. It brayed and turned to walk back into Wadi Kabir.

Rocio followed. At least the donkey knew the path.

FOURTEEN

The Storyteller

Rocio awoke and dragged herself out of bed for breakfast. The Old Library, or whatever the place was called, was deserted. Her father and Kenzie had already left; crept away like new conspirators. But they had left behind a breakfast to finish and to clear away.

When Rocio eventually found them, Kenzie and her father were already making marks on the ground at the spot where the lighthouse was to be. Kenzie was holding a handful of small stones and listening carefully. Rocio's father had some sheets of paper in his hand from which he was trying to show Kenzie something. Monkey was still perched on Kenzie's back. Luckily it was not an ape or an orangutan, thought Rocio. But then again, Kenzie was a big man. No, a small grey monkey was just fine. If she had a monkey on her back, she'd probably call him Jacko. Yet if she had a monkey on her back called Jacko then most likely she would not be called Rocio. You cannot change one thing without affecting change in another.

Her father waved to her as she approached. She saw that his face was animated, and enthusiasm sparkled in his eyes. They were at the stage he had been most looking forward to. It was an architect's dream.

'There,' he said pointing. 'Yes, right there.'

Luis Rodriguez Rodriguez directed Kenzie to place the stones on the center spot. Kenzie then handed him a stick he had been carrying. Rocio's father took the stick and made a large circle around the stones. He looked at his daughter and smiled. 'This is my *mundus*, Rocio. It signifies our world down here, upon the desert lands of our earthly soil.' Luis Rodriguez Rodriguez then placed the stick in the middle of the pile of stones. 'And this here shall be the center of the lighthouse. From here it will stand tall and reach up to connect with the heavens and with the movements and patterns of the cosmos. This wondrous lighthouse will be like a thread that creates a correspondence between that which is above and that which is below. Right here will be the base of our magnificent desert lighthouse.' Luis Rodriguez Rodriguez's face shone almost as bright as a lighthouse itself. Something was beaming through him and making him behave like a young kid. Rocio looked at Kenzie, who just nodded thoughtfully as if it all made perfect sense to him. Luis Rodriguez Rodriguez walked around the pile of stones three times. He pointed again at the center. 'Yes. This center, where the lighthouse shall stand, represents the single timeless present moment. This unmoving center is where time and eternity come together, and from this we shall bring light and wonder into the world.'

Rocio smiled. 'Sure, Papa, you know what's best.'

Luis Rodriguez Rodriguez nodded vigorously. 'Yes, yes. And this magnificent lighthouse will renew our connection with the cosmos above to bring the light of the heavens down here to shine through the darkness of our world. My dear, we shall renew our agreement with the cosmos and be no more the silent, deaf child amidst our starry brethren.'

'You sure know how to pick your words, Papa.'

'We had better get started. We don't want to leave the cosmos waiting,' added Kenzie dryly as he cracked a nut and gave it to Monkey.

Things had been agreed.

Kenzie set to work gathering the local builders and craftsmen. Recruiting was not difficult as everyone was keen to participate with the exciting, new project. The whole thing, after all, had been 'approved by Nur' as everyone kept saying. And in Wadi Kabir if Nur said that the sand was now pink, then pink it most certainly was – or one of various shades of pink. The people of Wadi Kabir were no strangers to argument, magic, or wonder. In fact, it was almost a part of their daily lives.

A makeshift hut was put up by the locals close to the construction area of the lighthouse. Inside the hut Luis Rodriguez Rodriguez would sit at his table going over the design plans. Mornings and evenings were the most useful times for work. Mornings were best because of the wonderful light that gave clarity to each inch of desert floor and each mud-brick. And the freshness too encouraged eager hands to do their work. During the middle of the day everyone rested. It was too hot to work. All the local people had their own rhythm, which meant siestas. Soon Luis Rodriguez Rodriguez began to remark how 'civilized' such siestas were. 'Rest is so under-valued' he would often say. Yet like in everything, there needs to be a balance. Rest would not be under-valued in a community that did nothing but rest. And rest is only real rest when it comes with a decent handful of work. Luckily for Luis Rodriguez Rodriguez and Rocio, the people of Wadi Kabir were good workers too, as well as being good resters.

In a land where everything is built from scratch, building a tower was no big deal. Nur had said that there had been towers in Wadi Kabir before, but they had been taken down when a previous local elder had decided that people needed to look more inward rather than skyward. But Nur was pretty sure that now was the time to connect the place to a new type of magic. She reasoned that people can only look inward if they have a decent connection to something that is also beyond them. And the lighthouse, she intuitively felt, was the right thing. If she hadn't had her own dream about the arrival of the father and daughter lighthouse builders, then she may never have suspected it herself. Such is the way things are oddly connected, especially when you least expect them.

Luis Rodriguez Rodriguez did not expect to see the arrival of a young man with a guitar.

'I'm going to sing your story,' said the young man, who looked to be about Rocio's age.

'Just you and your guitar?'

The young man raised his eyebrows in a sort of nonchalant gesture. 'I'll accept your ignorance with patience. It is not a guitar in my hands but an eleven-stringed oud. And upon this fine instrument I shall bring your story to the world.' The young man wriggled his fingers for a few seconds and then proceeded to pluck his fine wooden instrument. Luis Rodriguez Rodriguez had to admit it did sound good. Actually, somewhat better than good. The young man did not sing but instead clicked his tongue as he played. Luis Rodriguez Rodriguez observed this strange new apparition that had just arrived upon his construction site. He was thin, almost gaunt looking, and had a head of dark curly hair.

Some of the workers stopped to listen to the excellent finger-plucking coming from the young man. Shortly Rocio appeared on the scene and immediately came over to where the young man was playing. He plucked a few more notes and then abruptly stopped.

'Don't stop on my account,' said Rocio.

'I didn't,' replied the young man. 'I stopped when the music told me to. You may be pretty, but you don't have the power to stop music.' The young man looked at Rocio directly and did not divert his gaze.

Rocio wasn't sure if she had just been handed a sweet compliment or a sugar-coated insult. Either way, the best thing was not to think about it too much and to move on. Rocio was good at being practical at such things.

'And who are you, music maker?'

The young man gave a bow. 'They call me Amin. Amin the Troubadour. And I do not make music. The music makes itself, and then gifts it to me for my stories. I am a storyteller.' The young man again wriggled his fingers and began to play a few melodious notes. This time a few words flew from his mouth like escaping birds. 'I – am – a – storyteller – and – your - story – must – be – told…and – your – story – must – be – told.'

Amin's voice was as sweet as mead down a dry throat. It was intoxicating listening to him.

Rocio snapped herself out of her reverie. 'Not bad,' she said, hoping to repay the earlier ambiguous compliment.

Amin bowed again. 'Coming from your lips that was mighty praise indeed, which I do accept.'

Has he just twisted my words? wondered Rocio. Damn him!

'Okay, show's over!' shouted Luis Rodriguez Rodriguez. 'We have a lighthouse to build.'

'Exactly!' added Kenzie as he cracked another nut for Monkey.

Rocio had returned to the Old Library to take a nap. She was half-awake when she heard someone moving around. She soon found Nur moving from one room to another and shaking her head. The old lady with her long dark-grey hair looked frail at times yet still seemed to be invested with endless energy. She could walk into any home, building, or meeting in Wadi Kabir and no one would question it.

Nur spoke to herself. 'Still no books.'

'What's that?' asked Rocio.

'I said there's still no books here. I don't know why we call it the Old Library. We might as well call it the Absent Library.'

'I thought Kenzie was the Old Library. He has all the books inside of him.'

Nur threw back her head and laughed. 'That sailor boy! He's only got one book in him and it's filled with blank pages!'

'But I thought…'

'Don't think!' interrupted Nur. 'Thinking will get you to places that are hard to break out from. Now, come here.' Nur sat down nimbly upon the cushions of the room and took out a little leather pouch the size of her palm. Rocio went and sat down next to her. Nur opened the pouch and took out what looked to be a nail. She held it up for Rocio to see.

'A nail?'

Nur nodded. 'Yes, a nail. But it's not any old nail – it's a nail of love. And it has been filled with love for many, many years; more years than you've been on this earth, my child.'

'I don't understand.' Rocio gave Nur a questioning look.

'Of course not, I haven't explained it to you yet. Don't try to fly before you're given wings. Now, listen. This is *my* story. I was born into a noble tribal family in another region of this desert. Our family was the tribal leader and, as was natural then, we fought those of a neighboring tribe who attacked us. It was all warfare in those days – tribe against tribe. There was slaughter and bloodshed, as well as celebration and festivity. My parents were proud of what they had achieved and fought hard to maintain it. Other tribes were jealous, and we were forced to engage them in brutal fighting. Finally, our tribe all but wiped out our neighbors and forced them to flee further into the desert, in poverty and disgrace. It was forbidden for any of our tribe to mix or communicate with the enemy tribes. Ah, so it was in those days. And in my youth, I had the luxury of being protected and well provided for. One day everything changed. I remember this day as clearly as I see you now. Every week my mother would pass through the tribal settlement to visit her people, and often I would accompany her. On this particular day a ragged, emaciated woman approached us. My mother was immediately taken to compassion at this sight and asked if there was anything she could do to help her. At this point the ragged woman confessed to being the tribal queen of our enemies. On hearing this, my mother was angry for this enemy had dared to set foot into our own settlement. My mother screamed, 'You are the accursed slaughterers of our men – how dare you come here begging to me. Shame on you!' Yet the woman did not react in anger but with a look of pity. And these were her words to my mother: 'No, I did not come here for forgiveness, charity, or sympathy. I came to see whether your family had come to learn something from the deplorable behavior of our family. I do not wish to see the same fate that befell us to befall your family, for if it does then our children in this world will have no hope, and anger will spread like a contagion to infect all our futures.' Upon saying this, the woman turned around and left. I was deeply affected by that. After that time, I swore to myself that I would only seek a man of kindness to offer my heart to.'

There was a twinkle in the eyes of the older lady. She leaned over closer to Rocio.

'Not long after that I too was walking through our settlement and for some reason I began to limp. I felt a pain in my foot but didn't know why. At that moment a young man saw me and approached with great respect. He kneeled before me and asked if I would kindly lift my right foot just a few inches off the floor. I was surprised at the request yet did so for this young man seemed sincere. He reached underneath my sandal and pulled out a nail that had become lodged there. It was the nail that was causing me discomfort.' Nur held the nail up again for Rocio to see. 'And then the young man placed the nail into his little leather pouch and said – 'I shall keep this nail with me until my dying day for it has been a part of you, and surely contains more love than all the hearts of the desert." Nur gave Rocio a cheeky wink. 'Naturally, I went on to marry this charming man, and we left my tribe to settle here, at Wadi Kabir. And my dearest husband kept this nail in his pouch close to his chest for sixty years until his dying day, just as he had promised. Promises are hard to keep at the best of times. A promise kept for sixty years is one made from words of love.'

Nur placed the nail back into the leather pouch and then pressed it into Rocio's hand. 'Now, I wish for you to place this nail at the heart of the lighthouse, at its very center, for this lighthouse is special and so needs a special seed of love.' Nur stood up. 'In every story there is a song, and in every song there is a story, if you know how to listen. Good seeding, my dear.'

Rocio was left alone wondering about the nail of the heart.

The first circle of bricks had been placed around the pile of stones that marked the center of the lighthouse. Around the site men were laying mud bricks out in the sun to become dry and hardened. Rocio pulled her hat down over her forehead and went in search of her father. She found him inside his hut speaking with a couple of locals.

'Yes, wonderful – more mud bricks!' Luis Rodriguez Rodriguez was as animated as ever and seemed to be throwing himself into the project. 'But we need *something* to hold them together. You know – h-o-l-d t-o-g-e-t-h-e-r. Bricks need to be stuck, glued; they have to stick together.'

The two locals looked at each other and burst out laughing.

'What's so funny? This is a serious matter. If bricks n-o h-o-l-d, then lighthouse fall down.' Luis Rodriguez Rodriguez made a collapsing motion with his hands.

The two men were now in hysterics. Luis Rodriguez Rodriguez looked over at Kenzie who was standing nearby. One of the locals turned to Kenzie.

'Hey man, has this granpa here never heard of mortar?!'

Rocio too began to laugh, and it was then when she heard the sounds of gently plucked strings.

Outside the hut Amin was playing his oud. As Rocio came out Amin walked away toward the place of the lighthouse. He began to walk around the circle of bricks, changing the tune he was playing, and experimenting with different rhythms. Rocio walked over.

'Are you having fun?'

Amin strung on his oud. 'Enjoying myself and having fun are two different things.'

'Is annoying any part of your enjoyment?'

'No – but it is a part of the story.'

Here we go, thought Rocio. 'Okay, and what story?'

'As I said, I'm going to sing your story.' Amin played a few more notes.

'You are hard work; do you know that? Alright, why are you going to sing our story?'

'Because,' replied Amin in a melodious half-singing voice, 'stories need to be preserved and passed on. If there are no stories people will forget. And you don't want people to forget about this wondrous lighthouse in the desert, do you?'

Rocio sighed. 'But people won't forget. It will always be here – like the pyramids and the Sphinx.'

'Exactly,' said Amin with a smile. 'And just *why* were those monuments built?'

Rocio went silent.

'You see my point? We have the object, but we don't have the story. Humanity forgets too easily, and all that remains are stones. But if I put the history of this lighthouse into song, then it shall forever be passed on through future generations. A human heart *always* loves a song.' Amin smiled and began to sing…

And a vision he did have,
And a vision he did share
An architect and his daughter,
A morning dew so fair.

They made plans to bring the light
From the heavens to the earth,
A light so bright in desert sands,
A light from the heart to share.

…and he sang about a journey over the Sierra to where the waters of two different seas come to meet…

FIFTEEN

Never A Dry Well

L ife in Wadi Kabir was now centered around the building of the lighthouse. Tons of mud bricks had been made and were all dried out in long rows under the sun. The young people were excited and wanted to get involved with the grand, magnificent project. Many of them were carrying buckets of water from the local wells. Wadi Kabir was indeed a fertile spot in a dry land. There's never a dry well in Wadi Kabir, Nur had once said.

Luis Rodriguez Rodriguez was busy all the days and on-site during the construction. He was accompanied by Kenzie most of the time who helped to oversee the project. Luis Rodriguez Rodriguez was in his architect's world and Kenzie was in his as a man of the world. And the arrangement worked well between them. The center was gradually being built up, as those on the periphery looked on.

Nur gazed at the rising edifice. Maybe she had seen it already built long ago in her mind's eye. She seemed to be staring at it with a knowing look, as if the lighthouse was not so much *out there*, as brick upon brick, but rather as a lighthouse that rises within each of us and yearns to be switched on.

Amin the Troubadour circled the structure with his oud in hand, plucking and strumming and humming a tune. At times it looked as if the young, gaunt man was in his own daze. He sang not one note as the bricks began to rise. Instead, he was searching for a rhythm, a musical chariot to be the perfect vehicle upon which to send out the story of the lighthouse into the world. The young man only happened to sing whenever Rocio was in his presence. And Rocio, for her part, was drawn to the enigmatic minstrel despite her best efforts.

She pretended to be inspecting the brickwork as Amin came ambling around the circumference. Although he saw her he too pretended not to notice and did not meet her eye. However, by the next time he came around there was a song upon his lips.

And the waters of two colors they met
To guide to the shoreline ahead,
For two travelers be traveling from their land
To the land where sand flows upon sand.

And the singers of flamenco they met
To guide to the shepherd's way,
For two travelers be traveling by caravan
To the town where people forget.

Rocio's heart almost stopped beating. She tried to say something but only *erh* came out in a voiceless dribble. She turned around and marched away, letting her body carry her whilst her mind hung in some unreachable void. She went directly to find Nur.

Nur was in her little desert garden inspecting the irrigation flows when Rocio arrived. Nur took one quick glance at her and the corners of her mouth rose ever so slightly. *Humans and lighthouses, it's always the same thing,* she thought and gave Rocio a welcoming smile.

'My dear, what a pleasure to see you; water and youth are two of my favorite subjects and you've both arrived at the same time. Now that's certainly a good omen for the day.'

Rocio was taken slightly off-balance. 'Oh, that's good then. Talking of omens, have you been speaking with that troubadour guy, Amin?'

Nur raised her eyebrows. 'What's that got to do with omens?' When Rocio shrugged but didn't say anything Nur continued. 'Of course, I've spoken with Amin. I speak with everyone in Wadi Kabir. What kind of an elder would I be if I spoke with some people and not with others?'

Rocio wrinkled her nose, something she used to do more when she was a young girl. 'No, I didn't mean like that.'

'Then what *did* you mean like? I'm not a mind reader, my dear, despite what some people here may say.'

'Well, it's like Amin is singing about our own journey. He's saying it how it was – crossing the waters, the flamenco caravan, the journey to Shepherd's Way...I mean, it's like he *knows* it, but...but...but...'

'But, but, but – three buts in a row is a butbutbut.' Nur laughed at her own joke.

'Oh, Nur!' Now even Rocio giggled and the frustration fell away from her.

'Okay, my dear, you're surprised that someone else knows your story. What's the big deal? Everyone is going to know your story soon enough.'

'Be that as it may, I want to know how *he* knows now before the story's been told.'

'*He* meaning Amin?'

'Uh-hu.'

'Uh-hu meaning yes?' Nur gave Rocio an affected inquisitive look.

'Yes, well, Amin, of course,' replied Rocio trying to be deliberately casual as if the matter was not important.

'It's quite simple. Come here and sit with me.'

Rocio sat down beside Nur in the shade of several trees.

'Amin is a troubadour, a storyteller. And he is one of those special types of storytellers who make stories into myths so that they can live on, almost forever. And such myths have existed in the heart of humankind since the very first day. Myths are the carriers of eternal wisdom. And so, you see, your story-myth already existed even before you and your father acted it out. Everything already exists in potential in this creative reality of ours. A true troubadour like Amin is able to tap into these eternal stories and they flow into him. I can only guess that it was by seeing you and your father that triggered the connection to this actual myth. And rest, well, let's just say it was a download. Now do you see?'

'Sort of.' Rocio frowned. 'But that means that our story – our journey – is not original.' Rocio's face went sad.

'On the contrary, my dear. Your journey is so very original because it's the first one ever to take the potential of this story and to make it into something real – something *tangible*. And that's never been done before. It's the most wonderful act of creation to bring a cosmic story into being!'

Rocio's face brightened. She saw in her mind an endless spiral of letters swirling out of a black hole and into a galaxy to form spinning words as stars. These words continued to spin around and around, sparkling and fizzing like celestial fireworks. And then suddenly one of the stars broke up and all the letters fell through the star-sprinkled galaxy and into another black hole. And then they appeared through the dark orbs of Amin's eyes and drifted down upon his fingers. He wriggled his fingers and shook the letters into words, which then formed into sentences, and then into song, and then into a story about the most wondrous lighthouse of strange delights in the desert...

Luis Rodriguez Rodriguez was trying to prise a pencil out of Monkey's hand.

'He won't give it to you.' Kenzie cracked a nut and put it into his own mouth. Monkey gave him a disgruntled look and tried to break the pencil in half.

'Can't you control your own monkey?'

'He's not *my own*; he's a free agent. Monkey does as Monkey wishes.' Kenzie shrugged.

'But he always seems to obey you.'

'I've got the nuts.'

Luis Rodriguez Rodriguez left the room to look for another pencil. Rocio thought it was a good time to ask Kenzie a question she had on her mind. She entered the main room of the Old Library and sat on the floor near to the large, bearded man. Yes, his head could contain all those books, thought Rocio. Or maybe he is just a blank page after all.

'How's the building going?'

Kenzie looked across at Rocio and his face erupted into a broad grin. 'It's monkey-fantastic. We'll have that lighthouse up and running before the next camel is born.'

'Wonderful.' Although Rocio wasn't quite sure what it all

meant. It just sounded good. 'I was speaking with Nur recently and…'

'Wise woman,' interrupted Kenzie. 'Aye, that girl could spin a cloth with her knowledge that would cover the whole desert.'

'Right. Sure. And speaking of knowledge, she says that you haven't any books in you at all – that you're just one big blank page. What…'

Kenzie burst out laughing and threw a handful of nuts in the air. 'Aye, what a hit! She's spot on!'

'But I thought she called you the Old Library because of all the books you've read? I don't get it'

'It's all true, depending whereabouts in the story you are. I did have all those books in me; but Nur took them all away.'

'She took them all away, but how? I thought they were already inside of you?'

'Exactly. Already inside me, like everything is inside us. It's a total mess sometimes. A tragic novel here, a jealous story there; sometimes an angry book, other times a wishing and wanting fable. We're all so full of books – all up to here!' Kenzie brought his hand up level with his throat. 'But Nur knew how to take the books away; how to clean up my own library. And she took me right down to a blank page. Amazing…and now I'm creating a new book for myself, and it's going be the best story of all. Pulitzer prize stuff, I tell you!'

Monkey jumped onto Kenzie's back and nuzzled its head into the big man's neck. Kenzie cracked another nut and offered it up.

Rocio felt it was time to sleep.

Next morning a line of donkeys could be seen going back and forth from the well carrying buckets of water for the artisan builders who were crafting the blocks of bricks. Children were running around having a wonderful time amid all the excitement.

Luis Rodriguez Rodriguez was watching all this with a calm detachment. Never in his wildest imaginings could he have pictured this scene. How had he gotten here? It was such a far cry from the comfort of his own home. Where would he be now if he had never received that dream - still sitting at home? Why had it all happened to him? Too many *whys* and an over-abundance of *ifs*. None of it mattered any more. What did matter was that he was here now, and so was his daughter Rocio. And don't start something Rodriguez if you don't mean to finish it; that's what his father had always said.

By the time Luis Rodriguez Rodriguez arrived on site Kenzie was already busying himself with directing the construction. Everything appeared to be going to plan. This would never have happened so easily back home, he thought. Usually builders in Andalusia don't begin work until tomorrow… and tomorrow never comes. His papers and drawings were all laid out in his hut. For now, brick upon brick, something spectacular was being created from the ground up. Luis Rodriguez Rodriguez decided they didn't need him for the time being, so he left to go for a walk.

He took the track back into Wadi Kabir. As he left he saw Amin sauntering up to the lighthouse with his oud in his hands. As they passed close, Luis Rodriguez Rodriguez was sure he saw a flash of light dart out from the deepness of the young man's dark eyes. Or maybe it was just a reflection from the sun. The skinny young troubadour kept on walking, humming a rhythm through his partly opened lips, trancelike and seemingly connected to something in a very odd way.

Without realizing where he was walking he suddenly found himself standing near to one of the main water wells of the fertile oasis. He watched as a donkey came plodding up to the well and stopped there. Soon a little girl came skipping along and followed the donkey up to the well. She then turned the handle of the winch until a bucket of water appeared. She poured the water into a large skin bag strapped to the donkey's side. She then patted the donkey and whispered into its ear. The donkey slowly turned around and plodded off. It was then that the young girl noticed Luis Rodriguez Rodriguez for the first time. She smiled and came skipping over to where he stood.

'Hello. Are you the architect of the big light?'

'I am,' said Luis Rodriguez Rodriguez smiling.

'Then you are lucky, mister. There's never a dry well in Wadi Kabir.'

Luis Rodriguez Rodriguez nodded. That phrase was now becoming familiar to him.

'Yes, so people tell me. And why do you think that is?'

The little girl giggled into her hand. 'There's water because there's life. Where there's life there's water. Wadi Kabir is full of life.' The girl opened her arms as wide as she could. 'There's every life here – there's the life you see and the life you don't. Is your big light going to make us all see the invisible life?'

'Sure, I hope so,' replied Luis Rodriguez Rodriguez scratching his cheek. 'I'm hoping my big light will reach up high into the sky and bring down all wonderful things to see.'

The girl clapped her hands excitedly. 'Will the big light reach the stars?'

'Oh yes. It will reach into the starry heavens and bring light to other planets.'

'Yesss!' said the young girl in a high-pitched voice. 'And will it connect us to all the things that fly between the stars?'

'Oh yes. All of that…and much, much more.'

'Wowee…!! It's going to be a great big light!' The girl jumped around and skipped away clapping and singing to herself.

Luis Rodriguez Rodriguez felt like his heart was now beating not only for himself but for many other bodies too. He felt it pumping away inside of him as if it had to give blood for every living connected thing. And that was it. He suddenly got it. That was what it was all about…the big light…the well…Wadi Kabir…the caravan…it was all connected to the same thing, and it was beating inside everyone's chest.

Wow, it's finally happening...it's true – there's never a dry well in Wadi Kabir.

Rocio thought it sounded like a crazy idea. But then again, if an idea sounded crazy it was probably something she should listen to. So she did. She followed the donkey through the oasis, walking behind it slowly as it plodded past the people. Some of them waved to her. Rocio was now a regular and welcome sight in Wadi Kabir, and the locals treated her as one of their own. There she was, a European lady walking slowly behind a donkey through the dusty roads of a desert oasis. Nothing unusual about that. At least the donkey didn't think so, for it kept on plodding, knowing very well that it was being followed.

And eventually Rocio found what she was looking for.

Luis Rodriguez Rodriguez looked up from his resting position. 'Ah, you found me. Sorry, I was just taking some time out. How did you know where to look?'

'Oh, I followed a donkey.'

Her father nodded. 'Makes sense.'

'Why did you want to be near the well, Papa?'

'Well...I don't know. I just; well, I just found myself here. But that's great, isn't it?'

'Is it?' Rocio was beginning to feel a tinge of puzzlement creep in.

'Sure it is, because being here helped me to finally get it.'

'Get what, Papa?'

'Why there's never a dry well in Wadi Kabir.'

'Yes, I've heard that too. The people here say it often. I think it comes from Nur who said it first.'

'But don't you get it? That's exactly it…water is the water of life. There's so much life here. It's not the water they're referring to; it's the well of the human spirit – of the human heart. Here, the heart is full. And that's what we need; we all need to be full. But the world is full of dry wells, and the world is becoming drier and drier. We need *this* water, Rocio – the water of life.'

Rocio took her father's hand. 'That's your story, Papa, and that's why we're both here. The lighthouse is going to be a part of this fullness. It's going to bring a special light. Isn't that right, Papa? I know it's why we're here.'

Luis Rodriguez Rodriguez gently stroked his daughter's cheek. 'Yes, my dear, that's why we're here. And the big light at the top is going to restore the heart of the world. It's going to be wonderful.'

And the donkey brayed.

Soon the same little girl returned to the well.

'Mister architect, you still here?

'I seem to be.' Luis Rodriguez Rodriguez noticed that the girl was not smiling or looking joyful anymore. In fact, it was the total opposite. Her face was drawn into sadness and her eyes were tightened into little dark pinholes.

'You think you bringing the big light?' The little girl's voice had also dipped into a lower tone.

Luis Rodriguez Rodriguez nodded.

'My tiger tells me it's not true. He says you lie - that your big light fail. He says it all confusion.'

'What do you mean?' Luis Rodriguez Rodriguez looked confused himself.

And so too did Rocio. 'But there are no tigers in the desert?' The little girl stomped her foot. 'My tiger is my friend. Nobody sees him but me. He always tells me truth.'

'Ah, now I see. Well, maybe your friend the tiger is confused himself.'

'No,' blurted the girl. 'He right and strong. And he say there no big light. Your light just cloud of dust. That all – just cloud of dust say tiger.' The little girl kicked into the sandy ground, spun around, and ran off.

Luis Rodriguez Rodriguez frowned. Rocio fell silent. And then the donkey brayed again.

SIXTEEN

The Big Light at the Top

adi Kabir was a hive of activity. The locals had begun talking feverishly about the lighthouse, and all ideas and opinions on the matter were flying around the oasis. The excitement was rising and with it came a camel load of expectations, which was not lost on Luis Rodriguez Rodriguez. Kenzie, for his part, had been hard at work every day directing the construction and overseeing the local builders. Luis Rodriguez Rodriguez made sure he was present to check over every new section of the sixty-two-foot brick tower. It rose ever higher into the sky, almost like a human hand reaching out for the heavenly connection in the starry dynamo of light. Some of the locals said it represented the hand of humanity protruding from the desert floor and straining for the spirit of the skies. Yet there were others too who seemed less enthusiastic. Whispers circulated in the cool corners of dusty retreats that perhaps the lighthouse was another projection of humankind's ego, and that it would be struck down like some of the towers of old. As in all matters that were human, tongues wagged, eyes observed, ears overheard, and hearts were expectant.

As for Luis Rodriguez Rodriguez, he knew that sixty-two feet was not *that* tall. It could always go taller. But then where would you stop? Everything can always be bigger, longer, taller, wider, faster, etc. Wasn't that why the Tower of Babel eventually collapsed, because nobody could agree? His lighthouse was not about going higher and higher and farther away, but rather was about bringing something in. Luis Rodriguez Rodriguez's vision was not to reach *too far* – it was to bring a light into the world. And he knew you had to start with a fixed plan, and to finish it through. It was not important what other sizes the lighthouse could be – it only mattered what it was. Real function came from real design. The rest was just human greed for going that little bit more…

Amin the troubadour was also present every day, playing his oud to the rhythms of work. He too became a fixed presence in the daily life of the lighthouse of Wadi Kabir. He was the heart and soul of the story, and his nimble fingers plucked their tunes as the workers placed brick upon brick. They soon got used to his tuneful, wandering steps. Sometimes the workers used to stop and chat with him and share their own stories – sometimes not. Yet day after day Amin would play his oud and create himself into his very own story. After all, it is said that nobody exists outside of the shared story that is humanity. Everybody bathes in the same waters and swims in the same light that makes the world visible.

And Rocio continued to observe it all from a distance. She would watch the comings and goings as the lighthouse was raised higher and higher. This project had become increasingly important for her, even though she knew that its vision and completion belonged to her father. Yet she couldn't help but feel the butterflies in her stomach as she watched the bricks arrive layer upon layer.

With a curious expression she would also watch Amin as he circled the tower composing his odes and channeling a story in song through the wriggle of his nimble fingers. She felt a little funny too, knowing that someone else – a stranger – knew her own intimate story. And if she couldn't hide her own story from the eyes of the world, what could she keep hidden to herself? Was there no place that was hidden from the light?

On most days Rocio liked to stop by to see Nur and have a chat. It always seemed like a good thing to do, for some reason. And like usual Rocio found Nur between the water and the earth, under the shade of her trees yet within the warmth of the sun.

'You seem to have it all!' said Rocio as she approached.

Nur shrugged. 'That's just your own wishful thinking projected onto me. I only have what I have, and it's not much but it's all I need, thank you. The thing with you people from yonder is that your life is too cluttered. When you see simplicity you immediately think it's idyllic. Not having much to you is a good, simple life to me. And having to live within one's means is not idyllic; well, it's just plain common sense. You know what's wrong with common sense these days?'

Rocio shook her head.

'The problem is that it's neither common nor makes much sense to people these days, that's what!' Nur laughed at her own joke, which she did often.

'Yeah, I guess so,' replied Rocio in a low voice.

'You seem preoccupied; what's on your mind this time? Are you still lingering over that troubadour?'

'No, it's not the troubadour. It never was!'

'Yes, of course – *we* know that.'

'Nur!' Rocio realized she had suddenly raised her voice. A blush of embarrassment bloomed upon her cheeks. 'No, it's the light,' she said quickly.

'It's all about the light I guess. We can't escape that. Shall we go inside, my dear?'

Rocio followed Nur into the house and waited as the elder lady boiled a pot of mint-sweetened tea. Around the walls and niches of the house were various ceramic objects of different shapes, sizes, and colors. They appeared to be geometric shapes. Nur noticed Rocio's interest.

'They're all pieces of a grand mosaic,' she said as she took the pot off the boil.

'For what?'

'It's all part of the bigger story. Everything fits together, even the small parts. Every shape and size has its place in the mosaic of our lives, and these ceramics remind us of that. And so, your question on light?'

Rocio hesitated. 'It's nothing really. Only that since being here I've come to realize that everything is connected in ways I never thought. What I mean is that everything is connected, no matter how far away it is.'

Nur nodded. 'Like the ceramics you've just been looking at. It's all part of the grand mosaic, just like stories and light.'

'Exactly. Stories seem to be known, and fit into each other, and no one part can be totally hidden from the other. Everyone can reach into them to read them and find out. And then there is the light that…'

'Whooh, slow down and take a breath!' Nur chuckled and poured them both a glass of steaming, sweet tea.

Rocio breathed in deeply and took a sip of tea. 'If the light comes to the lighthouse, where will it truly come from, do you think? And will it be able to reach everywhere? Papa seems to have the idea that the light will reach everywhere, and not just this spot in the desert. Is there enough light for that? What do you think, Nur?'

A smile crept over Nur's face as she nodded to herself. 'Don't you go worrying about the light, my girl. There is light everywhere – even in the deepest darkness there is an abundance of light. And when you truly need it, it shall come…'

Nur opened her hand and at exactly that moment a ray of light fell into her palm and shone like a glimmering, sparkling ball. She then abruptly clenched her hand into a fist and the shimmer of light disappeared.

'I saw a child carrying a light,' Nur whispered in a soft voice. 'I asked her where she had brought it from. She put it out and said: 'Now you tell me where it is gone.''

Rocio then realized that some answers are not found in letters or spoken words.

Luis Rodriguez Rodriguez was explaining to Kenzie how the sun would provide the light. Kenzie was nodding abstractly as if his mind was wandering between the halls of a ruined mansion looking for wondrous gems in the dust.

'Yes, the sun, the sun. It provides all the light we need,' repeated Kenzie absent mindedly.

'Are you listening, Kenzie?'

Kenzie nodded.

'Kenzie!'

The large man suddenly opened his eyes wide. 'Sure, I got you, buddy! But someone has to find all the bits to put this thing together.' Kenzie wrung his large hands together as if he had discovered a plan within those halls and rooms of the ruined mansion.

'Put it all together?'

Kenzie nodded. 'Aye. I'm going to bring the sun down for you and make it radiate out as if it were a fizzling star. How's that for you, mister architect?'

'Splendid.'

Rocio cast a glance over the lighthouse as it rose above its sandy floor. It looked even more magnificent than she had imagined it to be - because it was real. It was not a glimmering white tower like most water lighthouses. This was a terrestrial lighthouse, reflecting the browns of the earthly soil. Its feet were planted firmly upon *terra firma*. In time it would grow its roots downwards into the bacterial gut of the earth. It could be no other way. What reached up into the starlit heavens also had to mix with the dirt and dust of the ground. One was not balanced without the other. It was not a fairy light, an immaculate conception of cleanliness. It was a desert lighthouse – a mass of mud atoms entangled within a body of brick amidst the grit of human need. And the world was in need of such a lighthouse. Nur had been right. But would it work...?

'Okay everyone, this is what we need!'

Kenzie's voice boomed over the desert air. Rocio looked across to the shed where there was the usual mix of activity and noise.

'That's right,' the voice boomed again. 'Find me non-coated copper wire, some glue and tape, some pieces of glass, a high factor sunscreen, some tea candles, a cup, a coffee filter, and some iodine. Oh, and does anybody have any blueberries?'

Blueberries? Rocio wondered why Kenzie would need some blueberries. Yet, she supposed, building a lighthouse in the desert had its own strange requirements as well as its delights. She could at least contribute the high factor sunscreen. Then there was…

Rocio was interrupted by the melodious notes of song as they danced against the desert sands. The words floated over to her as if they had been transported by the dainty hands of desert devas.

And in the town where people forgot,
In the land of those who are blind
There was one who saw with pebbles bright
The road ahead to find.

With dates and pebbles in hand
He did show the way to yonder land
Where those who guard the shrines by day
Are also blind by night.

Amin the troubadour wandered past Rocio with his oud cradled in his arms as if it were an extension of himself. The tune was now beginning to seep inside of her body, sailing through her cells and along the capillaries of her heart. She had to admit, it was an incredibly addictive tune. Damn you, Amin!

She looked at the young, thin troubadour as he sauntered near to her. He seemed lost amidst the tapestry of his own tune. Then she noticed there was something different about him. She didn't know what it was at first; there was just something different. And then she spotted it. It was his face. He was no longer gaunt. His face had become fleshed out as if filled by the nourishment of tune and the blood of song. He looked handsome, in an odd troubadour sort of way, thought Rocio. His deep-set orb eyes now shone with songs that sang of a distant earth.

Amin wriggled his fingers and continued with his tune. The melody vibrated with his step as he wandered close to the brick lighthouse. Rocio also went in closer to hear the melodious tune as it tangoed with the desert - one step, two step…She was longing to hear her own story.

> *Yet he who speaks by falcon's voice*
> *Is a true guide of the desert dunes,*
> *And with camels four he did deliver*
> *His guests by silence, time, and tune.*

And when they came to Wadi Kabir
They met with an elder pure and fair
To see their vision made into stone,
To see their dream made clear.

Rocio felt the lighthouse rising within her; constructed from cells and nodes and circled by rivulets of pumping blood.

'Ah, it's going to be just beautiful.'

Luis Rodriguez Rodriguez walked over to greet his daughter. 'And not long now; Kenzie is working on the light. Soon the big light will sit at the top of our lighthouse and it will shine forth forever.'

'Forever, Papa?' A questioning look rippled over Rocio's face.

'This wondrous lighthouse is not an object like some flat, two-dimensional block of stone. No, it is a call burning in our hearts, and with this call we shall restore the heart of the world.' Luis Rodriguez Rodriguez was speaking with such enthusiasm that his hands were waving about like a philharmonic conductor. 'We are restoring the transcendent once more into the mundane – this is the difference between the sky and the heavens. This is the difference between the dust and the soul of the earth. Look! Look, Rocio, at the beauty of the lighthouse. It's beautiful because it exists in both you and me. It exists in all of us. And it exists in every particle of the world too. Isn't that transcendent beauty?!'

Rocio had to agree. It was hard to disagree with such enthusiasm. And it was harder to disagree with the feeling of the lighthouse growing inside of her own body, just as her Papa had said. Soon a big light would be added, and perhaps that too would shine inside.

With books, books, and no more books
They met a friend cleaned out inside
Who with monkey, nuts, and an active mind
Could help them build their dream in time.

And so through song and story clear
Came He who sings these words to Thee
To help create this myth-ol-o-g-y
To last in stone for et-er-ni-ty.

And so came He too, to cast a spell of song over the deep well of Rocio's heart…to last in stone for…?

SEVENTEEN

Strange Delights

A wave of increased excitement and nervous energy rippled through the dusty streets of Wadi Kabir. Everybody knew the time was fast approaching when the great lighthouse would be turned on and it would be seen if a great light shone forth from the heart of their oasis. It was an open secret that Nur was planning a celebration to mark the much anticipated and greatly expected 'magnificent inauguration.' It was an event which had already united not only the people of Wadi Kabir but also people from further afield. Deserts were places where not only the sands moved and spread around, but also the words and whispers coming from the human tongue.

The grand lighthouse in the desert had become a favorite topic passed from mouth to mouth along the desert caravans. All the surrounding communities now knew of the wondrous tower being built in Wadi Kabir by a certain architect known as Sidi Moustache and his daughter, Morning Dew. And the rest…well, the rest was like the words of a song dancing upon the plucked strings of an oud.

The desert winds had carried tongue-twisted tales of human hubris building a tower to reach the Creator in the skies. Other stories spoke of attempts to bring the sun down into the earthly desert. Some people's tongues wagged of magic and sorcery, whilst others spoke of mystery, ambition, crazed love, and the great longing of a heart once broken. Could the once broken be restored? Curiosity in the desert was now at desert-fever pitch.

Nobody knew the exact date of the inauguration, when the big light at the top of the lighthouse would be turned on. Yet that didn't seem to matter. As it has been said, in the desert time moves in its own circles. It doesn't move in the circle of a clock-face, or the tiny circle of the watch strapped to a nervous wrist. Desert time doesn't move in five days on and two days off like the artificial weeks that make up the artificial years that people generally grow old by. No – desert time moves more like the wind when it whistles through the branches of a tree. As the leaves rustle, they learn of the ways of the world and the antics of the human species. And then they let out a great sigh. Time in the desert moves in great sighs.

And like the leaves of a tree, the people in the desert knew that the sighing was getting lower, and slower, and thus the great day was approaching. They set out in their own caravans toward the now almost mythical oasis of Wadi Kabir. As the trails, tracks, and caravans of travelers descended upon the oasis, so too did the whispers spread amongst them.

Could it really be true? Why a lighthouse in the desert? everybody wondered. Would it really bring its light into the dark places? Incredulity, the mark of humanity, fueled the other mark of humanity - curiosity. Debate raged amongst the travelers as they met upon the way. Tongues wagged, hands wavered, and minds fettered over all the impossibilities and the possibilities. The desert sands vibrated under the stampede of so many questioning souls.

The people of Wadi Kabir had also been quick to make use of this once-in-a-lifetime opportunity. Clay replicas of the lighthouse started to spring up across the oasis in the hands of entrepreneurial sellers. Cool, dusty shop interiors were now adorned with stacks of clay lighthouses of all different sizes. Some of them could be fitted into the pocket or held in the palm of the hand as a lucky talisman. Others had a hole at the top where the light should be, and a coarse string pushed through so the lighthouse could be worn around the neck. All kinds and variations were now being proudly displayed across Wadi Kabir. Nur had not been amused. Clichéd human traits, she had said when first discovering the phenomenon. Yet like any wise elder she knew that the people could not be denied the right to make a living from all such situations that life might throw in their path.

Makeshift stalls had also appeared in several locations. More than one could be seen in the square near to the water troughs where camel riders came with their thirsty camels. They were also placed at the corners were dusty tracks met and crossed. And least surprisingly of all, close to where the desert arrivals were pitching their tents on the rim of the plateau where the famed lighthouse stood.

'Papa, we can do this, can't we?' Rocio and her father Luis Rodriguez Rodriguez were sitting together in the peace of the construction hut. For once it was empty of people. Kenzie and all the lighthouse workers were outside making the finishing touches. Luis Rodriguez Rodriguez had wanted to spend a few quiet moments with his daughter before everything became catapulted into a frenzy of final activity. He looked into the pure eyes of his one and most beautiful daughter.

'We have already done it,' he said with a smile. 'It's already been achieved. It was completed before we had even begun our journey. It only needed to be actualized in *this* world – in *our* world. And that was why the vision came to me that night whilst I was sleeping. It whispered to me - *Luis Rodriguez Rodriguez, you must awaken and do this. If you do everything else in this world, yet do not do this one thing, then you will have done nothing. But if you do this one thing, then no matter what else you do in this lifetime you will have done everything.* And then it whispered one more thing. The voice said – *it's already been done. The light shines*

— now it must shine through you and your daughter, Rocio. The light can only shine if there is another light in the human heart that reflects it back. So you see,' said Luis Rodriguez Rodriguez, his face reddened by toil under the gaze of the sun, 'we are here to return a missed call to the cosmos, and to say 'Sorry I was out when you called – but I'm here now – I hear you and I'm listening!"

'Yes, Papa – you really are an architect. But it's not buildings that you design, it's…'

'Hey, we got it up!' Kenzie's voiced boomed into the confined space of the hut. 'You just have to come out and see this. Aye, she's a delight – a pure delight she is!'

Luis Rodriguez Rodriguez and Rocio stepped out upon the desert plain. In front of them towered their dream – a glorious sixty-two-foot lighthouse.

'Sixty-two feet,' whispered Luis Rodriguez Rodriguez softly.

'Aye, plus the big light at the top,' added Kenzie. Sure enough, there at the top of the towering edifice was placed the orb of an eye that appeared to be shimmering with the reflected shards of sunlight. 'She's soaking up the sunlight now. Let's give her a few days and then she'll shine all through the night, every night – for eternity.

'She's so beautiful.' The words had barely left Rocio's lips when the melodious words of song blossomed forth like spring buds.

And where there is light there water be
For one never finds a dry well here,
And with hearts that look deep inside
There is a light that shines without any fear.

And this great light of the human heart
Was placed upon the stone of earthly dirt
For where there is darkness within our realm
There is a light that lasts for et-er-ni-ty.

Amin the troubadour plucked the strings of his instrument as one would gently caress the first stirrings of the heart.

Rocio could not stop herself from blushing. Amin's robust, youthful face shone with vigor and energy. Words were whole worlds where many new emotions were colliding. Atoms were like droplets that were rearranging into new forms which one day may learn to sing, and dance, and love.

Later that evening Rocio and her father had been invited to eat with Nur at her house. As they walked under a beautiful evening sky, Rocio gazed at the trinkets of stars that were dotted overhead. She stumbled and almost fell over flat on her face upon the dusty earth beneath her.

'Hey, watch yourself!' said her father. 'Are you tripping over

Amin the troubadour?' Luis Rodriguez Rodriguez smiled to himself.

Rocio pinched her father's arm. 'Papa, stop it! I just like his songs - that's all! Anyway, I was looking at the stars. I was trying to find Aldebaran.'

'Aldebaran?'

'The Hadji said that the star Aldebaran means *the follower*, and that perhaps she can help us to follow our own destinies.'

'Mmm,' muttered Luis Rodriguez Rodriguez.

'I wonder what Aldebaran will be thinking of us now. What do you think, Papa?'

Luis Rodriguez Rodriguez took his daughter's arm and linked it through his own. 'I'm sure the fair Aldebaran will be smiling down upon us. We are awake, Rocio, and that means our destinies are before us. We shall walk one step at a time.'

After several more steps they arrived at Nur's house. It was a familiar mud-brick building much like the rest of Wadi Kabir. It was neatly arranged and looked after, as if displaying the orderly mind of its occupant. Luis Rodriguez Rodriguez and Rocio were ushered inside and into a candlelit room. Nur greeted them wearing an elegant dress. She may have been carrying many years upon her shoulders, yet Nur was graceful and agile, with a light that glowed within. The three of them sat down to eat.

They ate in respectful silence, sharing their company and the gentle presence of desert time. After they had finished eating a delightfully tasty and light mix of vegetables and rice, Nur called for the obligatory pot of steaming mint-sweetened tea.

'People have already begun to arrive, and many more will come,' said Nur as she broke the silence between them.

'There will be many?' Luis Rodriguez Rodriguez gave a questioning look.

'Enough.' There was a short pause. 'Light attracts many things. It brings strange delights as well as the fluttering moths of the night. Many people will be bringing their disbelief, hoping to witness your failure. Others will be bringing their fears at what the light might expose to them. Everyone brings something which is a part of their self. No one walks alone, or empty. A true light reveals many things. That is the way it has always been. We can sink into the material darkness or reach for the sparkling light. Humanity can go one way or toward the other. And as for our dear Earth; well, she patiently cradles us, waiting for her children to grow up.'

'Many…' Luis Rodriguez Rodriguez spoke quietly. He wasn't sure if he liked that thought. He had never planned for a large audience. It wasn't supposed to be a spectacle. But then again, perhaps he shouldn't have been so naïve; people are people after all, and everyone likes a good spectacle. And in the desert, it was no different.

'Our part?' Rocio's voice was both quiet and questioning.

Nur reached out and patted Rocio's hand. 'Yes, our part as the redeemer. It's the part where we restore the connection that has been lost, to bring back meaning to our world once more. We are here to join that which should be joined.'

'But why us? I mean, my Papa and me are just normal people.'

'No one is *just normal*,' replied Nur with a playful gaze. 'And it's not just you either – it is all of us. Real things must be explained through people and not through the darkness. Humanity has been placed in the midst of darkness to demonstrate by its own light the existence of a greater light. It is by this greater light that our attention shall be called back to all that is sacred in this cosmos and within our own hearts. As proof that we can restore our humanity, we must first restore the light all around us.'

'And the lighthouse will do this?' asked Luis Rodriguez Rodriguez.

Nur nodded her head in a slow and thoughtful manner. 'It is one of many; just as you and I are one of many. This has been going on for many, many years; more years than our history can remember. The signs of this are all around us. We have innumerous objects scattered around our landscapes for those who wish to see them. Sadly, an ignorance permeates our world like a mist and hides these obvious signs from our eyes. This wondrous lighthouse of strange delights is one such sign. And by its light it will help people to see. One day perhaps humanity will see what it has always known, and that day will change all our destinies forever. But for now, we must follow *the follower.*'

Nur looked across at Rocio and a star sparkled in each one of the elder's eyes. Rocio felt as if she was beginning to understand even if she couldn't put it into words. But that was okay, she didn't need the words just yet. Besides, even in the silence she could feel the melodious strings of a story-in-song shimmering within her.

The three of them were sitting outside of the Old Library. Kenzie would now and again break a nut in the palm of his hand and give it to Monkey. Kenzie wasn't a man of too many words. At least not since his internal library had been wiped clean. The three of them – or rather four if you include Monkey – knew that different days were coming. Perhaps they wanted a final quiet look at the stars together before it all began.

'I never thought it would come to this.' Kenzie spoke first, letting his baritone voice break out over the still, night air. 'All my travels have brought me here. Who would have thought it? Not me…not me. But thanks for everything.'

Luis Rodriguez Rodriguez and Rocio both knew he wasn't speaking to them, nor thanking them.

'No one can guess it ahead of time,' added Luis Rodriguez Rodriguez. 'We're guided to where we eventually end up. And yes, thanks for everything.'

'And may a star be your guide – thanks for everything.' Rocio felt a great warmth well up inside of her.

'Marvelous,' said a voice. Everyone turned to look at Monkey. Had Kenzie thrown his voice? Surely not. Monkey took another nut from Kenzie's hand and popped it into his mouth and crunched down on it. 'Marvelous,' said Monkey, picking his nose.

EIGHTEEN

The Light and the Darkness

Several days more had passed and still the tents kept arriving. Out in the desert they formed a ring of onlookers, each with their own supplies of food. They were prepared to wait for as long as was necessary. It is certainly not every day that a lighthouse in the desert gets turned on. In fact, if we are to be honest about it (and honesty is a good choice right here) then this was to be the first time any such desert lighthouse was going to shine its light over the sands. Deserts don't often get their very own lighthouses. Maybe this will change in the future once people realize what an excellent idea it is.

Luis Rodriguez Rodriguez opened his eyes as a ray of light entered the room and hit the mud wall. He felt an emptiness in his stomach. He knew that the day had finally arrived. And for a few moments he couldn't move. His body had become frozen, leaden and heavy. There was something lurking around, but he just couldn't seem to know where. Maybe, he thought, it was the young girl's tiger stalking him. The unknown, invisible tiger of the night seeking to eat the light. *Tiger, tiger, burning bright in the forests of the night – are you here to steal the light?*

At breakfast Luis Rodriguez Rodriguez was exceptionally quiet, which meant that he was just that bit quieter than usual. It didn't take long for Rocio to notice her father's mood. 'What's up, Papa?' She popped a piece of hot baked bread from the morning's fresh delivery into her mouth. She watched as her father raised his left eyebrow. Ahh, the left eyebrow, thought Rocio. That meant that something was worrying him. 'Are you worried about today?'

Luis Rodriguez Rodriguez stroked his lips. Ahh, the lip stroke, thought Rocio. She knew her father must be anxious. She leaned over and patted his knee. 'It's okay, Papa. Everything is going to be exactly as it should be.'

Ahh, the reassuring but not one-hundred-percent-sure knee pat, thought Luis Rodriguez Rodriguez. Yes, it was going to be one of those days when things happened the way things had to happen.

The rest of the day stretched further and slower than usual for desert days. Time appeared to be almost at a standstill. Luis Rodriguez Rodriguez wished to spend some time alone.

227

He wandered through the lanes of Wadi Kabir that were now busy with excitable people and raised chatter. As soon as people saw him their voices hushed, and their eyes followed him. Luis Rodriguez Rodriguez didn't like being the center of attention. *This is not about me; it is about the light, about the light.* He repeated over and over silently within. His legs were taking him without the guidance of his eyes. He was being steered by reflexes and not by thought or intention. When he next looked up he was standing at a busy corner of Wadi Kabir at the edge of where the local market was in full, daily swing. Vegetables, fruits, and food stuffs were being haggled, bought, and sold like on every market day. Yet this time Luis Rodriguez Rodriguez noticed that others were walking through the market carrying boxes brimming with clay objects. He looked closer at the boxes as they passed. They were flogging lighthouse figurines! Boys, girls, men, and women – the lighthouse sellers were from all ages. All that was needed now, he thought, was Monkey to come along selling.

He turned away and quickly left the bustling market and headed for shade. He wandered into one of the cafes of Wadi Kabir where time was experienced between sips of tea and coffee amidst tobacco smoke. Right now, even tobacco smoke was welcomed as long as it didn't come with a lighthouse trinket. Luis Rodriguez Rodriguez took a seat in the corner and accepted the tea in a chipped glass that was placed in front of him. At the next table two men were playing a rapid game of backgammon. They threw the dice and moved their counters the instant the dice had shown their dots. It was as if they knew their moves in advance and were just waiting for the predictable sets of numbers to fall. Whatever dots landed face up, the options were limited. Luis Rodriguez Rodriguez watched several games pass in fascination. When the match had finished, and one of the men had taken the victory, Luis Rodriguez Rodriguez took the opportunity to lean over.

'It's amazing how fast you both play. You seem to move without thinking.'

One of the men shrugged. 'Years of experience,' he replied in a casual voice.

'Experience without understanding is water without wetness,' replied his opponent.

'A fish can only drink so much of the sea,' added the first man just as quickly.

The two men looked at Luis Rodriguez Rodriguez yet said nothing else.

Luis Rodriguez Rodriguez finished his tea and left.

Back at the Old Library the architect with the vision, the famed Sidi Moustache, sat quietly on the bench outside.

'There you are, Papa!' Rocio came over and sat down next to her father. She handed him a freshly cut piece of watermelon.

'Some things just taste better in the desert'

The only thing left to do was to wait until the night time. Light needs the darkness just as much as boats need water, or birds the air. Like most things of the world, a light really comes into its own purpose when it is given something to shine against.

Back out on the plateau the city of tents was stretching further and further. A mixture of brown, cream, and dirty, desert-curdled white canopies stretched across the sands. The smell of food was drifting over, mingling with shouts, laughter, cries and cackles. The scene had all the hallmarks of a festival. All eyes were now focused upon the desert edifice. They were awaiting the creation born of a vision from a crazy European architect known locally as Sidi Moustache. This grand story had been told over and over. And just like every other story, this one also attracted its commentaries.

But there are no boats in the desert — why do we need a lighthouse?

Lighthouses are for water, not for sands. Let the sands swallow up this affront.

It's an anomaly — it doesn't belong here. The dunes will soon cover it over, or the desert winds will knock it down with a fury.

Why should the desert accept an outsider? We should only listen to our own.

We don't need light — we need money. Give us money!!

It's all crazy...let's watch it fail. We're not the stupid ones...

And the voices kept on drifting over the spires of desert tents, whilst others were silently spoken inside. Something within each person was mesmerized by the curiosity of the unknown, and the potential for strange delights.

As the darkness began to fall Luis Rodriguez Rodriguez became increasingly nervous. Who wouldn't be in his shoes? And his daughter Rocio too felt the same nervous expectation dwelling within her. It had all come to this. The path had brought them here. And this wouldn't be the end either – it was only the beginning. It's just that to arrive at new beginnings you first have to finish previous roads. And this road had very clearly stopped for them at Wadi Kabir. An onward road would surely be beckoning or calling out in song. But first...

...first, the light had to shine in the dark.

Anticipation rose through the oasis and the surrounding desert sands. Everyone in Wadi Kabir had turned out in their best evening clothes. There was a colorful array of bright dyes and exuberant eyes. It was an enchanting display of excitement, eagerness, expectation, and bundles of joy all wrapped into the gleaming bodies of people. Hawkers were mingling with the crowds, *Get your own lighthouse – Wonderful lighthouses – Good luck Lighthouses...*

Children were running around, soaking up the waves of excitement that were now rolling over everyone. All the young ones knew something special was about to happen, and that this 'something special' would be talked about for evermore in the days of the desert. Yet beyond that the young minds knew little else. And the older minds too. Many of them were anxiously expectant, uncertain of just what was about to happen. And even if the lighthouse did shine its beam across the desert sands – then what? Would it help the camels to steer their passage? Maybe, but camels always know their passage through the desert. Surely a lighthouse would not alter this?

So many unknowns.

Nur kept a cool composure. She knew it had all happened already; and now the whole thing just needed to be actualized. She didn't particularly like that word *actualize*. It sounded too methodical – too mathematical. Yet words were all she had to try to transmit just a little of what she knew deep inside. Maybe next time, if there is a next time, she would leave it all to the song, or so she thought. Nur looked over to where Amin the troubadour was making his seemingly final paces around the sixty-two-foot lighthouse. It seemed that he too was waiting for the final words to come through, riding upon the crest of rolling rhythms and spiraling strings. The cosmos is forever in movement, waiting for the rest of its parts to catch up.

Rocio caught up with her father and squeezed him close. 'Whatever happens tonight, I want you to know that you've done something incredible. I'm so proud of you, Papa.'

Luis Rodriguez Rodriguez took his daughter's hand and kissed it. 'And I want you to know that from the very beginning, when you looked at me with your pure soul and said to me 'Okay, Papa, let's make it happen,' that a universe exploded within me. And that universe is you, and your love. And this lighthouse is just a small fragment of my love for you. And if just a speckle of your love is within this light, then whoever this light falls upon will be blessed, as I have been. And that is something worth sharing, is it not?'

Rocio blushed. Her father had certainly changed. He had, she felt, finally become the person he had always meant to be. And that made all the difference.

Night fell upon the people of Wadi Kabir, and upon the surrounding sands. It was the night they had all been waiting for as it was a night without moon or stars in the sky. The engulfing darkness was waiting for its light.

Kenzie gave a nod to Luis Rodriguez Rodriguez and the two of them walked over to the base of the lighthouse.

'This one's for you, buddy,' said Kenzie. 'You know what to do. Aye, it's been a grand pleasure. I reckon working with you has been my best book yet!' Kenzie gave Luis Rodriguez Rodriguez a slap on the back and walked off.

Silence fell over the surrounding area. Even the children had stopped running around and were now staring over at the wondrous lighthouse, joining the rest of the gazing faces. Luis Rodriguez Rodriguez knew that it was now or never, and now was always going to be better than never. He looked over at Rocio who had been joined by an elegantly dressed Nur. Rocio smiled and nodded.

He pulled the switch.

There was a hiss. And then a crackle. A low glow emerged from the top of the lighthouse. A light was struggling against the surrounding darkness.
*Come on, come on…*whispered Luis Rodriguez Rodriguez under his breath.

Let there be light, whispered Rocio quietly to herself.
Nur looked up into the deep, dark night and frowned. She suddenly felt something in the air, and it didn't feel right. She instinctively put her arm around Rocio as if to protect her.

It seemed to Luis Rodriguez Rodriguez that the light at the top of the lighthouse was struggling against some invisible force. High up there, sixty-two feet above, the light and the darkness were clashing.

And then he felt it. Slightly at first, brushing against his neck. Was he mistaken? Then it came again, this time stronger. No, he hadn't been mistaken. Something like a tiger's breath had brushed against him.

Nur gripped harder against Rocio.

'What is it?'

'Something is rising in the desert,' replied Nur in a low, sullen voice.

'What does that mean?'

'I hope it isn't what I think it is.'

What's that?' asked Rocio nervously.

Nur gave a strained expression. 'The desert fury. And it comes quickly. Be prepared to move, fast.'

Now others had begun to feel it. It started with a low gust of air that moved through them like a slithering desert snake. And then it grew stronger. A sudden gust slapped against the tents and a loud boom echoed out.

'It's the Fury!' shouted a voice.

Then people began to panic. They ran in all directions. Some ran towards their tents and others away. Parents grabbed their children and fled leaving their food sizzling upon their small desert fires. Within moments a large exodus of fleeing people had formed and was heading for the center of Wadi Kabir.

Nur had already grabbed Rocio and was running with her in locked arm back toward the oasis.

Luis Rodriguez Rodriguez stood in shock. He didn't know what was happening. Where was his light? He looked up again to search for his glow when a hand of sand slapped him squarely in the face. He fell backwards upon the floor. The next thing he knew a large human hand reached down and grabbed him. He was pulled up and pulled along as a howling desert wind began ripping across the plateau. The last thing Luis Rodriguez Rodriguez remembered hearing was shrieks and human cries. His eyes were almost closed as sand particles punched into his skin with a fury. Everything else was a haze and a dusty blur.

NINETEEN

The Desert Fury

The place looked like a disaster zone. Far into the horizon swathes of colored tents lay mangled and strewn across the desert. Items of belongings were ripped, broken, or buried never to be found again. People were strolling like lost shells upon the newly shifted sands. Nothing in the desert stays the same for long. Change is the only constant reminder. And a desert fury can never be reckoned with.

Kenzie had taken Luis Rodriguez Rodriguez to shelter at Nur's house, where Rocio was waiting. In the morning their sullen faces caught the new sun but did not reflect it. Their deep sadness absorbed the bright rays as a sponge and their eyes stared vacantly ahead of them.

Luis Rodriguez Rodriguez shook his head. 'I don't understand.' Nur was quick to reassure. 'There isn't a great deal to understand about the desert except that the desert is Master.

When it wishes to blow, it blows. And we all have to accept it. The desert cares little for human intentions and plans. There was nothing we could have done. The desert fury came and that was that.'

'Yes, Papa,' said Rocio softly. 'Nature has her own ways too.'

'It was the tiger,' mumbled Luis Rodriguez Rodriguez.

'The what?' Nur squinted.

'The tiger,' he repeated. 'The little girl's tiger had predicted the lighthouse would be struck down into a cloud of dust.'

'The only tigers here belong to the imagination!'

Luis Rodriguez Rodriguez wiped his hands down over his face. 'All those people! They came for the lighthouse. They were expecting the light to shine.'

Nur tutted. 'Don't you be worrying about other peoples' expectations. They'll get over it.'

Luis Rodriguez Rodriguez looked at his daughter. 'I'm sorry, my dear. I thought it could be done.'

Rocio took her father's hand in hers. 'Don't be sorry, Papa; it's not your fault. It still can be done.'

'How?!' The older man's voice croaked.

'By clearing up the mess first.' Nur stood up and left them to finish their breakfast.

Out on the plateau it was not a pretty sight. Kenzie crushed an already broken miniature clay lighthouse under foot.

'Didn't need those things anyway!' he muttered gruffly.

He gazed out over what was left of the sixty-two-foot edifice, and it was now significantly shorter. Well, he thought, at least half of it is still standing.

Back at Nur's house Kenzie sat down next to a despondent Luis Rodriguez Rodriguez.

'How is it?' Luis Rodriguez Rodriguez wasn't sure if he wanted to know the answer to his own question.

'Which do you want first – the good news or the bad news?'

'Give me the good first.'

'Well then, the lighthouse is half-full.'

'Mmm. And the bad news?'

'The lighthouse is half-empty.'

A smile slowly appeared upon the architect's face. 'So, I guess all is not lost then?'

Kenzie slapped him on the back, though this time more lightly than usual. 'Nothing much is lost, my friend. Just time, energy, a few mud-bricks, and a pocketful of enthusiasm. And there's more from where all those came from – right?'

Luis Rodriguez Rodriguez nodded slowly. 'Yeah, I guess so.'

Rocio went with Kenzie to see the lighthouse. Her father had not wanted to leave the shelter of Nur's house. He did not want to meet the faces of the disappointed people. Luis Rodriguez Rodriguez felt that he had let them all down; that somehow the desert fury had been his fault. That perhaps the storm had been a sign that he had done something wrong. If only he could find out what it was.

On the plateau a crowd had gathered to look at the ruin of the lighthouse. Rocio stayed close to Kenzie, more for not wanting to get lost in the chaos than anything else. Although she could not understand the words being muttered around her she could guess what they were saying. The desert tongues were speaking of the failure of the 'wondrous lighthouse' and how it had all been a mistake from the start. Suburban hands, they would say, have no part in desert affairs.

But it was not our hands we built with – it was our hearts.

Rocio could not help but feel the sadness and confusion. She experienced an overwhelming sense of bewilderment. Even those who expected the lighthouse would fail only imagined a non-glow or a faltering light. No one thought the desert fury would arise so quickly and so unexpectedly. Normally there were warnings. The desert people always somehow sensed in advance its arrival. This time everyone had been taken unawares. The people of the desert blamed themselves more than anyone else for this lack of foresight. Amidst this self-admonition no one seemed to take notice of the European architect and his daughter. Their vision for the lighthouse may have failed but it was at the hands of the desert; it was no fault of human hands. Naturally, there were some who considered that the desert fury was a sign of the desert's anger against the intrusion of the lighthouse. Yet these voices preferred to remain mostly quiet amidst the labor of locating lost belongings and gathering the torn tents. It was a spectacle that should never have been, and that was that. The desert people felt fools for having allowed themselves to be drawn into such a charade. They were practical people – dreams and visions were for idle minds or for the soft heads of outsiders who have yet to be scorched into sense by the desert sun.

Rocio bent down and picked up a broken fragment of a miniature lighthouse left behind from the previous evening's chaos. She then took a fragment from the fallen lighthouse. She placed both pieces together in her hands - the original and the copy – and their likeness caused in Rocio her own confusion. She turned to Kenzie who was close by.

'Why are the false and the true so similar?'

Kenzie stepped over and took both Rocio's hands in his own large, hardened hands. He looked at the two mud-clay fragments. 'Aye. But they're of different scale. For those who are attracted to the copy, they have no need of the original. Most things in this world are a copy. It's the same with us, girl. Most of us are but a copy, and we don't have much interest in seeking out the real.'

'Everything sounds like a spectacle.' Rocio let her hands drop away and the broken fragments fell back onto the sandy ground.'

Kenzie nodded. 'Aye, that it is…that it is. But things such as this should not be a spectacle. The light was the light.'

Kenzie took Rocio by the shoulders and gently steered her away from the crowded plateau.

Nur remained within the now half-shadow of the lighthouse. She had been busy all morning helping her people organize and clear up the mess. The inhabitants of Wadi Kabir had turned out in full force, dressed in clothes ready for work. Their elegantly colored clothes of the evening before had been stored away again, awaiting the next grand celebration, wedding, or fiesta. For now, it was back to practical matters. The drab shades of the desert returned to deal with the sand, dust, dirt and dryness.

Still, in Nur's mind all was not lost. Setbacks were just a part of life. They are obstacles, nothing more. Nur and the people of Wadi Kabir helped their desert neighbors collect their belongings and shared with them plentiful water. After all, there is never a dry well in Wadi Kabir.

Over at the far edge, on the opposite side where the lighthouse stood, Nur noticed a solitary figure. It was that of a lean, young man.

Amin the troubadour looked on thoughtfully. His eyes took in the full scene slowly and carefully. He looked up and down the remains of the once wondrous lighthouse. He seemed to be nodding to himself. Even in the ruins there was a song to be sung. His long, thin arm reached over and pulled out the oud that was hanging across his back. He then wriggled his fingers as if calling forth the energy of momentum and motion. And then the fingers struck the strings.

Nur could not hear the tune for she was too far away. Yet she watched as the young man concentrated upon his task. And then it dawned on her why this troubadour was so important. This young man had recognized his task. And he continued with it.

Rocio was sitting under a tree in Nur's garden, protected by its shade. It was like a mini-oasis within an oasis. The water flowed through the irrigated channels to soak the roots under the dry earth. Beside her sat her father. He had hardly spoken a word all day. Rocio knew that inside he must be questioning every action, every motivation, and every wish. He was searching for the place which held the error. But maybe there was no place where the error could be found. What if it was not an error but something else…

'Papa?'

Luis Rodriguez Rodriguez didn't say anything, but he made a gentle turn of his head to show that he was listening.

'You still believe in your dream, in your vision, don't you?'

Her father sighed.

'Your vision is the *real* thing, Papa. It's not this.' Rocio opened her hand and within her palm was a small, undamaged clay miniature of the lighthouse. At the top, where the great light was supposed to be, was a hole for the string to go through. 'See, Papa. This is what people were celebrating. But your dream is still real – it always was.'

Luis Rodriguez Rodriguez took the small, clay lighthouse from his daughter's hands and turned it over in his fingers. 'It has a hole where the light should be,' he said in a low voice.

'Exactly.'

Luis Rodriguez Rodriguez laughed. He didn't mean to, he just did. And he kept on laughing. He laughed until his eyes and cheeks were wet. 'It has a hole where the light should be,' he again muttered as he finally managed to hold back the laughter.

Rocio grabbed her father's arm and snuggled into his shoulder. Her own cheeks were also wet and salty, with the trickles of laugher and love.

Shortly afterwards, Nur came strolling up to the house. She was not alone. Beside her walked the lean figure of Amin. They were both in conversation, although as they arrived Rocio could only hear soft tones floating past like pieces of driftwood. The surprise at seeing the young troubadour jolted Rocio into an upright position. She nudged her father.

Nur waved a hand at them. 'Don't bother getting up. I only want you both to listen to the song.' Nur approached the shade of the tree and sat down next to Rocio and her father. 'I'd like you to listen to how the song continues.' Nur nodded over at Amin, who raised the oud and immediately plucked the strings as if old friends.

His melodious voice floated out, cutting through the dry heat…

> *Yet when the hand did pull the switch*
> *The light of eternity did not arise.*
> *In its place the desert fury unleashed*
> *And sent people fleeing in shouts and cries.*
>
> *The lighthouse was struck by the fury of sand*
> *And cut its height in half to the ground.*
> *The Light it did struggle against the Dark*
> *Amidst the confusion of the human Heart.*
>
> *The people they did disperse far and wide*
> *Back to their lives amidst the desert dunes.*
> *Whilst others fled, others remained,*
> *Their task at hand now firmly engrained.*
>
> *A time for soul-searching is now at hand*
> *As time awaits upon the land.*
> *The lighthouse again remains for human heart*
> *To be in service to the greater part.*

The last vibrating note of the oud flittered into the branches of the tree where it nestled against the leaves. Amin lowered his head, yet not before stealing a quick glance from Rocio.

Nur waited. 'Don't you hear it?' she said finally.

'Hear what?' asked Rocio. Her gaze swung between the elder Nur and the singer of the song.

'The story tells us the way forward. Listen again to the last verse.' Nur nodded over at Amin who once again unleashed his mellow voice.

A time for soul-searching is now at hand
As time awaits upon the land.
The lighthouse again remains for human heart
To be in service to the greater part.

Luis Rodriguez Rodriguez looked at Rocio. It was obvious that neither of them was getting the drift of what Nur was trying to tell them. Rocio shrugged.

'Well then,' said Nur with a smile, 'I will have to spell it out for you two youngsters. Like most things in life we need the right ingredients; just like in cooking if you wish to have the right kinds of food to eat. And in life these ingredients are often the right people, the right place, and the right *time*. We have the place here, at Wadi Kabir, and the people here and you two,' she said pointing at Rocio and her father, 'but it seems we didn't have the right time. The song tells us this - *As time awaits upon the land.* The time is still waiting for us. And the lighthouse waits for us too, but in a very specific way. It waits for us *to be in service to the greater part.* Don't you see it?'

This time it was Luis Rodriguez Rodriguez who shrugged. 'Many people came together in this project for the spectacle.' Nur shook her head. 'This was partly my fault. I should never have allowed it. The lighthouse, or rather the light you are bringing to the world, is a service – it is not a fiesta.'

Rocio noticed that Amin was looking over at her and smiling. He nodded his head slowly. '*Their task at hand now firmly engrained.*' He spoke the words like a song.
'How did you find it – the song?' she asked.
Amin looked down before replying. 'I don't find anything. The song always finds me. But only if it wants to be found. It's always their song. I just pass it along.'

All eyes were now on Luis Rodriguez Rodriguez. Slowly he got up from his sitting position and without saying a word quietly walked away.

TWENTY

A Different Rhythm

The whole place was still and quiet as if listening to the whispering of the stars overhead. Luis Rodriguez Rodriguez searched for Aldebaran in the night sky. Perhaps it is true that no task is ever made easy. He had thought that arriving at his destination would have been enough. He thought it was the journey that was the trial, and that the actual building was the easy part. So much for his own expectations, he mused.

The architect known as Sidi Moustache strolled over to where the remains of the lighthouse stood. As Kenzie had said, it was now only half-full, some thirty feet or so left of its cylindrical body. He reached out and touched its brick curvature. It felt cool now that the rays of the day's sun had left it alone. Yet Luis Rodriguez Rodriguez was sure he felt a slight hum coming through the bricks. He put his ear to the brickwork. Yes, sure enough, it was there. The lighthouse was humming faintly to itself. It was as if a continual heartbeat was reverberating throughout the edifice. The lighthouse remained alive, he was sure of it. And it was speaking softly to him. Luis Rodriguez Rodriguez remained for a long time with his face and arms pressed against the cool bricks. *I don't understand* he whispered. *Tell me what you need me to do.*

Very early the next morning Rocio awoke to the sound of movement. There was shuffling and muffled voices going on in the Old Library. Then nothing. Rocio's head had hardly touched the pillow when she was asleep again. Later when she rose for breakfast she noticed that the place she now called her 'desert home' was, in fact, quite deserted. She ate alone, wondering where her father and Kenzie could have gone to. After breakfast she decided she would go for a stroll through Wadi Kabir. It was time to mingle and to be seen again, she thought.

The frenetic activity of the past few weeks had gone. Everything, it seemed, had returned to its desert normality. The locals were back on the streets in their djellabas or wearing casual loose-fitting clothes. The regular market was bustling, and the local bakeries were serving their warm, flat bread. Even though there was activity, movement, and transaction, there was still an air of peace that Rocio sensed. She stood at the corner of the market area and observed the comings and goings. Then she realized what it was – it was the rhythm of life. Life here in the oasis had a different kind of rhythm from anywhere else she had experienced. There was busyness and yet there was a slow, unhurried rhythm to it. Observing and sensing this rhythm made life back home seem that much more artificial.

'It's okay, miss Rocio.'

Rocio turned around to see a lady with a wrinkled face standing behind her.

'Sorry?' said Rocio in her polite European way.

'It's okay. Everything happens in its own way. Don't fight against it. Work with it.' The older lady smiled, displaying a half row of yellowed teeth, and walked off with a bunch of green herbs under her armpit.

Rocio decided it was a good time to visit Nur. Then again, any time was a good time for visiting Nur as far as Rocio was concerned.

She didn't even have to go as far as her house. Rocio saw Nur standing at the end of her dusty track observing the people of Wadi Kabir passing by. Nur greeted Rocio with a wide smile as cheery as a sunlit embrace.

'A fine day for Wadi Kabir,' said Nur as Rocio came up to her. Rocio gave the elder lady a hug. 'A fine day? Even after all that's recently happened?'

'*Especially* after all that's recently happened,' said Nur with a penetrating gaze. 'The amazing thing about life is that it just keeps on going. Some people don't try to get back up, of course. But those that do just learn a bit more about how to keep going.' Nur nodded over onto the main dusty road

ahead of her. Rocio stood and watched for a while, joining Nur in quiet presence. It took her a while but then she noticed. Every now and then one or two men would shuffle off down the track that led away from the oasis and toward the plateau where the lighthouse stood. Nur put her hand on Rocio's shoulder. 'And I got rid of all those lighthouse charms. We don't need those toys around here. We have the real thing.'
Rocio sighed. 'We *had* the real thing.'
Nur laughed. 'Come. Let's see how life just keeps going.' The elder started off down the track and Rocio followed.

Someone had given Luis Rodriguez Rodriguez a hat woven from palm leaves to keep the sun from his head. Kenzie was wearing a disheveled 'desert explorer' type of hat. They were both tying together a corner of the hut. Two other men were helping to put back together the 'Architect's Place' as they called it. The desert fury had completely destroyed the previous one; this was version 2.0.
'So this is where you both are!' Rocio approached the hut. 'Papa, you didn't say anything this morning.'
Luis Rodriguez Rodriguez looked up from his work. A concentrated expression was etched across his face. 'You were sleeping. I didn't want to wake you.' And then in his eyes shone a twinkle, just like the old days. Rocio smiled. She noticed also other men around the place who were collecting and gathering up the fallen bricks. They were walking off with boards full of bricks upon their shoulders.

'What are you organizing here, Papa?'

Her father shrugged. 'I'm not organizing anything. I came here with Kenzie to mend the hut. The others just came. I didn't tell them to do anything.'

'So what's going on?'

Luis Rodriguez Rodriguez gave another shrug of his shoulders. 'Life goes on, I guess.'

Kenzie nodded as if to reconfirm the statement, then went back to fastening his corner of the hut.

'There's never a dry well in Wadi Kabir,' said Nur softly.

The donkeys were back in operation. There was no fanfare, cajoling, shouting, or laughing as before. There was only the quiet, reassured, concentrated work. No one needed to be told anything. It was as if the first time around had been a test run; a beta-lighthouse prototype. Now the real work had begun.

Rocio helped bring refreshments to the workers, as well as looking after the donkeys. She especially enjoyed looking after the donkeys. They also reminded her of Nash and their travels together from the Sierra mountains and across the watery Straits. Those days seemed so far away now. The desert sun had burnt a different time and memory into her features. She often thought back to their time with the Hadji. Rocio knew without a doubt that they had not journeyed alone. What they were doing now was for everyone. It was not *their* lighthouse – it was a lighthouse for the world. Even Monkey came over and accepted a nut from her hand. Wow, thought Rocio, things have changed.

Monkey gave a whooping noise as he cracked the nut and popped it into his mouth. 'Marvelous,' said Rocio under her breath.

As Rocio was on her way to the well she crossed the path of Amin who was carrying a load of bricks. As they passed they briefly halted. Rocio was surprised to see the lean man with something other than his treasured oud in his hands.

'You're not seeking the song anymore?'

'The song will seek me when it is ready. For now, there is a different work to do.' Amin gave a slight nod and went on his way.

Even when he was speaking out of song, Rocio could hear the chimes in his voice as if the words were strung as a set of melodious bells. She caught her mind drifting into lands she didn't dare to venture. *Stop it, silly girl!* She told herself. *Desert boys and Andalusian girls don't mix.*

The previous weeks had been condensed into days. A distinctly different rhythm had entered life around the lighthouse. There was a harmony that had not been present in the same way before. The feeling and joy of the fiesta, the spectacular show that had permeated the building of the first lighthouse had been replaced by a serene and dedicated sense of work and service.

Wadi Kabir was no longer the talk of tall stories, magical myths, and expectant extravaganza. It had fallen into ridicule and rebuke, head-shaking, and I-told-you-so's; which was really in the best interests of Wadi Kabir. It was now a desert place left alone to get on with its own thing. Stories of the rebuilding of the lighthouse only met with incredulity and doubt. The lighthouse was now protecting itself. The people of Wadi Kabir had come to realize that when a thing needs to be done then the best thing to do is to get on and do it. A genuine act does not need to be turned into a party. An unspoken trust grew up between all those who worked hard on the new lighthouse. And those of the oasis who were not directly involved tried to help in other ways. Maybe it was a donation of food, a cup of chilled water, a reassuring smile, a nod of the head. It was all there. Wadi Kabir had come together in an unexpected way like never before.

Nur joined Rocio and her father on the bench outside of the Old Library. It was the end of another day and the workers were tired. Kenzie had already retired to his room with Monkey in toe. Rocio heard the crack of a nut from inside and smiled.

'Kenzie really loves his Monkey.'

'We love those who understand us best,' replied Nur.

A silence fell over the three of them. There was no need to

speak if there was nothing more to say. Rocio looked up into the starry sky and breathed deeply.

It was some time later when Luis Rodriguez Rodriguez spoke. 'The lighthouse will soon be ready.'

'And so will the world,' replied Nur quietly.

Luis Rodriguez Rodriguez, Rocio, and Nur may have been thinking the same thought, yet no one said anything. It didn't need to be voiced. The only thing left to do was to finish the task at hand and to wait. After all, it was no longer in *their* hands anymore.

And somewhere deep down inside each of them this gave a feeling of relief, and freedom.

TWENTY-ONE

The Humming Bricks

The mud bricks, parched hard in the baking sun, were all now in place. The sixty-two-foot lighthouse looked similar to how it had stood the first time. Yet there was something different about it. Unnoticeable perhaps, although perceptible to those who came to stand close to the edifice. The lighthouse was now imbued with its distinct presence. As dusk fell, the coolness of the desert drifted in across the plateau. Gradually, the locals came one by one to give witness to the imposing monument. To some, it had become a friend. For others, a guardian of the oasis. There were also those who felt that the lighthouse was not of their world. The people who had given their service in work to the great tower now sat at its feet. They made a circle around the base of the structure and just sat in silence. Some had their heads bowed; others were looking up at the stars that flickered in and out of the surrounding darkness.

Luis Rodriguez Rodriguez and Rocio came out of the hut together. They stopped as they saw the workers gathered on the ground around the lighthouse.

'What are they doing, Papa?'

'I don't know,' whispered her father. He began walking over to the lighthouse with Rocio at his side. As they approached close, one of the men put his finger to his lips as if motioning to silence. Luis Rodriguez Rodriguez sat down to join them and cocked his head to listen. A blanket of moonlight had fallen across the plateau. Rocio gazed around her at the scene.

There was a spectacular silence. It was so very different from how it had been before. Now there were no children running around, people shouting and selling, families laughing, and food smells circulating through the air. Now there was starlight and silence.

Rocio chose a spot for herself, away from her father, and sat down upon the hard, sandy stone floor. She closed her eyes and quieted her mind. She stayed that way; not knowing or caring how time was dissolving and swirling past her. She stayed exactly where she was – *how* she was – until she heard it too.

A faint humming rose within her. It felt as if the cells of her body were gently vibrating. Without thinking she simply allowed the mild hum to pulse through her body.

When she opened her eyes again she saw that the gathering had increased in size. Rocio recognized the face of Nur several rows away from her. Like everybody else, the old lady had her eyes closed and a serene look upon her face. Many people were now quietly sitting around the lighthouse. It appeared that everyone had found their own hum. Then something moved in the corner of her eye. Rocio turned her head slightly to see a tall figure approaching the circle. The figure stopped and pulled something over his shoulder. A note was struck, and it reverberated across the plateau. Soon a mellow voice was carried upon the still desert night air…

Our human hands came here to work
To know the glory of sacrifice,
For those who come only to receive
Will find no light in the deepest night.

By silence did our toil endure,
A full oasis joined at the core,
Placing our faith in worlds beyond
That connect us to our Evermore.

Not by word of mouth or other sign
Did people gather by the base of the Light,
To open their hearts to the hum of the stone,
A peaceful retreat in the dead of night.

Now the rhythm beats to a different drum
And time calls us to follow her care,
The people are here upon her hour
To see the Light so bright and fair.

Rocio stood up and allowed her legs to carry her away. Far
away from the plateau and to where the edges of the desert
toyed with the night's shadows. She found a spot alone where
several palm trees were standing as sentry to the encroaching
sand. She leaned against one of the trees and lazily gazed into
the darkness. The tiniest of desert breezes touched past her.
Rocio was getting used to the distinct smells and silences of
the desert; in a strange way they provided their own comfort.
She wasn't sure how long she had stood there before she felt
a presence behind her. She turned and saw the now familiar
tall, lean figure of Amin the troubadour.

'Why?' was the only question that left her lips.

Amin approached to where Rocio stood. 'Your father will
switch on the lighthouse. You should be there.'

Rocio turned away. She tried to think back at why she had left
the gathering in the first place. She couldn't remember the
actual impulse. She just knew she had to leave.

'I don't think it's ready,' she said finally.

'Or you are not ready?' Amin spoke in a soft, mellow voice.
'People become confused over bricks, yet we are all here to do

the same thing. And in the end, we shall all go through the same thing. We all greet the same end.'

Rocio didn't say anything. It didn't seem to matter if she spoke or not.

Amin took a step closer. 'There are still secrets.'

'There are?' Rocio's voice was almost a whisper.

'Let me tell you one more.'

Rocio turned to fully face the young troubadour. 'You're going to sing it?' Rocio's voice couldn't disguise its tinge of irony.

Amin shook his head. 'This secret will be spoken.' Amin then leaned in and put his mouth close to Rocio's ear. His lips moved almost imperceptibly as if the fluttering of wings of tiny insects.

Rocio stepped back. 'That can't be,' she said, her voice faint.

Amin nodded.

Rocio knew she had to leave.

Luis Rodriguez Rodriguez came slowly strolling up the quiet sandy road. He could make out the seated figure of his daughter on the bench outside of the Old Library. He came up to the bench and sat down without saying a word. It was several minutes of desert time before anyone spoke.

'How did it go?'

Luis Rodriguez Rodriguez turned his head to face the side

profile of his beloved daughter. 'It didn't go.'

'What happened?'

'Nothing. I didn't turn it on.'

'But why not?' Rocio turned to face her father. His sun-darkened face still retained the softness she knew and loved.

'It wasn't the right time. We had the right place, but not the right time or the right people.' As he spoke this last word he placed his hand upon the hand of his daughter.

'Thank you, Papa.' Rocio leant her head against her father's shoulder. 'It's all been so much. I feel exhausted.'

'I know, sweetie. Me too; me too. It won't be long now.'

After a few minutes Rocio raised her head. 'Let's do it now!'

'What?'

'Switch on the lighthouse now, while no one is around. Let's just do it.' An eagerness had crept into Rocio's voice, and she experienced a sudden burst of energy. She squeezed her father's hand tightly.

Luis Rodriguez Rodriguez smiled. It sounded like a good plan.

Father and daughter walked together through an almost deserted Wadi Kabir. It was late at night and most people were in their homes for they rose early with the first rays of morning light. They walked in silence; two figures upon the dry earth.

As they came up to the lighthouse Luis Rodriguez Rodriguez once again pressed his hands and ear against the cool stone.

'It's here,' he said softly.

Rocio did the same and listened as the low hum caressed her cheek. She then stepped back and nodded to her father.

Luis Rodriguez Rodriguez stepped through the small opening into the interior of the lighthouse. He was now in its very center. For the second time he pulled the switch that activated the light panels.

'There you go,' he said under his breath.

Outside Rocio and her father gazed up at the tall brick tower that loomed before them.

'I think Mama would be proud.' A tear formed in the corner of Rocio's eye.

'I know she would be.' Luis Rodriguez Rodriguez put his arm around his daughter's shoulder. And they waited. They waited for the first glow to appear above them in the desert night sky.

But it never came.

They knew they had waited long enough. It was Rocio who was the first to turn around to leave.

'Come on. Maybe tonight was not the night.'

Her father turned to join her, and they began walking back to the oasis. This time more slowly than before. They walked down the dusty track that led away from the plateau. Eventually it opened out onto the main road that would take them back to the Old Library, and back to their sanctuary.

As they passed the track that led off toward Nur's place they stopped. Partway down the track they saw her. Nur was just standing there, her face lit up by the moonlight. She tilted her head upwards in the direction of the lighthouse. Rocio slowly shook her head in reply. There had been no light. Nur smiled and nodded back. It was a smile of strength. Perhaps she knew something that Rocio did not.

'Come on, Papa.'

They arrived at the Old Library in silence and went to their respective rooms. The days had been long, and Rocio was truly exhausted. Her body just needed to rest. As soon as she lay down upon the bed she was fast asleep.

The sound of cracked nuts woke her up. Or rather, to be more precise, she was awoken by the sound of nuts being cracked close to her ear by Monkey who was sitting next to her bed. It was late morning and Rocio had overslept breakfast. Monkey offered a sleepy Rocio one of his nuts.

'Thanks, Monkey.'

Monkey smiled; or rather he bared his teeth. But instead of leaving he decided to have a poke around the room. He shuffled across the floor and rummaged through the low wooden shelves that housed the few belongings that Rocio had. He held the pouch in his hand and looked at it.

'Monkey, please, no,' said Rocio sleepily. Then she strained her eyes. 'What's that? Monkey, can you bring it here?'

Monkey hopped over and gave the pouch to Rocio, who looked at it for a few seconds before the realization dawned on her. It was the leather pouch that Nur had given to her earlier; the one that had the nail of love inside.

'Oh, no.' Rocio slapped her hand to her forehead. She had forgotten to plant the nail at the heart of the lighthouse like she had promised. 'Oh, idiot me!'

Monkey chuckled.

Rocio reached out and gave Monkey a hug. 'Thank you, Monkey - you're brilliant!'

Monkey skipped out of the room. 'Marvelous.'

Rocio turned around. 'Who said that?'

TWENTY-TWO

When you Seed a Nail of Love...

Luis Rodriguez Rodriguez and Kenzie were sitting in the local café sipping tea and coffee respectively. It hadn't taken long for Rocio to find them. In such a place as Wadi Kabir, nothing takes long to find or to know. And if it does take long, then there's a specific reason for it. Rocio had no specific reason to delay in finding her father. On the contrary, she had a rush.

'Papa, I forgot it – but now I've got it!' she said in one quick breath. She was panting from almost running from the Old Library to the café.

'Whoah!' Her father lifted up a hand as if to slow down an avalanche of air.

Kenzie nodded. 'Yeah, I didn't get that either.'

Rocio held up the leather pouch in her hand. 'It's missing this. I'm sure of it! Look, can you both meet me at the lighthouse this evening, as soon as it starts to get dark?'

'Sure.'

'No problem.' Monkey jumped onto Kenzie's shoulder as if to secure the agreement.

'Great – see you both then.'

Rocio turned and left the café as quickly as she had entered

'Any idea on that?'

Luis Rodriguez Rodriguez looked at his large friend. 'Rocio does what Rocio does best.'

Both men nodded and sipped their drinks.

Nur had just stepped out from the schoolhouse when Rocio encountered her on the road.

'I've been looking for you!' Rocio was again out of breath.

'Well, now you've found me.' Nur gave a smile.

'I went to your house but you weren't there.'

'Because I'm here.' Again, Nur gave a simple smile.

'Yes, well. Can you come to the lighthouse tonight, when it gets dark?'

'Yes, I can. Anything you wish to tell me?'

'No…' Rocio hesitated. 'Err, yes. Don't tell anyone. I don't want a large group. Just the right people…'

Nur nodded. 'Of course.'

Rocio left and took the track leading away from the oasis and toward the plateau where the lighthouse stood. This time she didn't see any donkeys. When she arrived at the plateau she went directly to the Architect's Place, her father's work hut. Inside she searched for the tool she knew she needed. It didn't take her long to find it in a place that was stacked with tools. She then walked over to the lighthouse and without hesitating stepped through the opening into its dark, cool interior. The center of the lighthouse was a low room with a thick ceiling. Rocio knelt upon the dusty floor and with the trowel began to dig. It didn't take her too long to dig a small hole. Despite the coolness of the air her forehead was soon dripping in sweat.

'Yeah,' she said out loud as if talking to someone, 'I'm sure you like to see a person sweating.'

When she was finished she took the leather pouch out of her pocket and tipped the nail into her hand. She then carefully placed the nail in the ground at the heart of the lighthouse.

'This is the *mundus*, the center that connects the earth with the sky,' she whispered. 'From one heart to another - I hope it brings you the light.'

She covered up the hole with dirt and stood up. Suddenly she felt dizzy and her head began to spin. *Should've eaten breakfast… and lunch*, she thought to herself. She immediately sat down and rested against the bricks. A low hum seeped into her body.

When she opened her eyes again the bright light outside had faded. Dusk was approaching.

'I can't believe I've been asleep all this time.'

Nobody answered her.

Rocio pulled herself up and stepped outside. She was still feeling hungry, and tired, but that didn't seem to matter. A desert chill was coming in that sent a shiver through her body. She wondered if she had time to go back to the Old Library to wash, eat, and freshen up. No sooner had she had those thoughts when three figures appeared at the edge of the plateau.

Her father, Kenzie, and Nur approached and soon all four of them were standing close. Nobody spoke for a long drawn out pause. Everybody looked at each other as if knowing why they were there. Something then caught Rocio's attention and she turned to see another figure approaching. The silhouette of a tall, lean person approached. Nobody said anything until Amin the troubadour was amongst them, making five.

Rocio looked over at Nur. 'I didn't tell anyone,' said the elder lady.

'Nobody had to; the song told me,' responded Amin in his sun-tipped voice. He closed his eyes and a melodic flow of words dispersed into the night…

Now everything was finally set
With people, place, and time just right,
For the architect to pull the switch
And give the world its greatest light.

For once Amin was not accompanied by his oud. He sang only with the companion of the human voice and the music of his being.

'I can't argue with that,' said Rocio.

Nur laughed. 'Maybe it's about time you just let things be.'

Rocio looked over at her father who gave his daughter a tender look.

'Go on. It's your turn now to pull the switch.'

The dusk had quickly turned to night, and the darkness around them was still and heavy. The night was absent of sound, hanging like a void. And somewhere in this void was a longing for the light.

Rocio breathed in deeply as she tucked into the dark interior of the lighthouse where only a short while earlier she had been sleeping. Her hand reached for the switch.

'You know what to do,' she whispered softly. 'You can bring light to the world – we really are in need of it.' She thought she felt the bricks around her humming as if in response. Rocio pulled the switch. 'There you go!'

She felt a shudder pass through her body. Then she felt the chill again.

Outside they waited for Rocio to join them. She came out and went over to her father who put his arm around her shoulders and gave her a hug.

'That's my girl.'

And then they waited. Their heads were turned upwards and their eyes searched for the light. And then…

Above the heads of the five gathered figures a low light lit up upon the top of the lighthouse. Soon all of them could hear the humming as it grew in strength. As the humming increased so did the glow of the light. Then suddenly a bright flash shot out from the peak of the lighthouse and bathed the surrounding darkness in a magnificent beam of light. As the light slowly began to rotate it lit up things in the deepest night that had until now lain outside the reach of the human eye. Luminescent creatures swam within the beam of light, floating and swirling like magnificent desert divas. Small desert dragons flapped their sand-sprinkled wings and cascading waterfalls of kaleidoscopic hues irradiated the night sky. The colors were coruscating, contracting and expanding. And then the energies within the light shot out in all directions, reaching to touch the places where ignorance partly clouds peoples' hearts.

And within the river of light that poured over the desert there were many other things too, and yet only for the eyes of each beholder. Each person saw only what they could see – those innermost dreams, desires, longings, and wishes that fill us all throughout our lives. As Luis Rodriguez Rodriguez had known, the lighthouse in the desert was not for the visible things of the world but to show people those things that they ordinarily *don't see* but long to see. For such things are the truth of any person's life. The lighthouse of the desert was a light for the human heart, and not for the eyes. The light would shine forth for each person to see what was truly dwelling within them. And then in turn each person would become their own lighthouse, shining out into their everyday worlds. A lighthouse in the desert is one, yet the light within each person is many.

'If someone turns on a light in the darkness, from the brightness of that light will spring up many wonders.' Nur spoke in a crisp, clear voice so everyone could hear.

'When you seed a nail of love…' Rocio's softly spoken words trailed off into the desert air.

'Aye, she's a beauty.' The low, baritone voice of Kenzie boomed into the night. Everyone smiled. It was then that Luis Rodriguez Rodriguez noticed that for the first time Kenzie didn't have a monkey on his back.

'We've just restored to the world something that is very, very old. Something that we all carry within us' Luis Rodriguez Rodriguez smiled and then gave silent thanks deep within.

The final words of the song were spoken from the lips of the young troubadour:

And the star did shine far and wide
Touching those upon distant shores
For when you turn on a light in the dark
The greatest wonders are for evermore

And then Amin stepped close to Rocio and placed his mouth against her ear. He whispered so softly that only her inner ear could make out the falling patterns of his words - *Yes, when you shine a light in the dark, The greatest wonders are for evermore...Oh, the greatest of wonders, Are for ev-er-mo-re...*

Rocio knew that Amin had saved the very last verse for her alone. It was the only gift that he had left to offer her. Songs and love were the only things that filled him. It was then that Rocio realized there was no going back because a true heart always takes you forward, and ever deeper, into the very center of where one needs to be. A quiet voice from inside her opened up for the very first time, to spread the gentlest of warmth needed to thaw the early morning dew.

Luis Rodriguez Rodriguez lifted up his head to the stars. 'Thank you.' The words came out and swirled to join the creatures of the light amidst the cascading currents of colors. 'The world has a new song – a *song of songs*.' Nur reached out and touched Amin gently on his arm. 'And tomorrow at dawn you shall sing the song of songs for everyone in Wadi Kabir. Now we must share this with others. We must share the song and the light.'

'Yes,' replied Amin. 'Yet there is one last verse that is needed to complete the song.' He looked over at Rocio and his eyes told the full story. He was waiting for a response, as if waiting too for the very heart of the cosmos itself…knowing that love is the true light that we each bring to the world.

For when you turn on a light in the dark,
The greatest wonders are for evermore…

The Song of Songs

And a vision he did have,
And a vision he did share
An architect and his daughter,
A morning dew so fair.

They made plans to bring the light
From the heavens to the earth,
A light so bright in desert sands,
A light from the heart to share.

And the waters of two colors they met
To guide to the shoreline ahead,
For two travelers be traveling from their land
To the land where sand flows upon sand.

And the singers of flamenco they met
To guide to the shepherd's way,
For two travelers be traveling by caravan
To the town where people forget.

And in the town where people forgot,
In the land of those who are blind
There was one who saw with pebbles bright
The road ahead to find.

With dates and pebbles in his hand
He did show the way to yonder land
Where those who guard the shrines by day
Are also blind by night.

Yet he who speaks by falcon's voice
Is a true guide of the desert dunes,
And with camels four he did deliver
His guests by silence, time, and tune.

And when they came to Wadi Kabir
They met with an elder pure and fair
To see their vision made into stone,
To see their dream made clear.

With books, books, and no more books
They met a friend cleaned out inside
Who with monkey, nuts, and an active mind
Could help them build their dream in time.

And so through song and story clear
Came He who sings these words to Thee
To help create this myth-ol-o-g-y
To last in stone for et-er-ni-ty.

And where there is light there water be
For one never finds a dry well here,
And with hearts that look deep inside
There is a light that shines without any fear.

And this great light of the human heart
Was placed upon the stone of earthly dirt
For where there is darkness within our realm
There is a light that lasts for et-er-ni-ty.

Yet when the hand did pull the switch
The light of eternity did not arise.
In its place the desert fury unleashed
And sent people fleeing in shouts and cries.

The lighthouse was struck by the fury of sand
And cut its height in half to the ground.
The Light it did struggle against the Dark
Amidst the confusion of the human Heart.

The people they did disperse far and wide
Back to their lives amidst the desert dunes.
Whilst others fled, others remained,
Their task at hand now firmly engrained.

A time for soul-searching is now at hand
As time awaits upon the land.
The lighthouse again remains for human heart
To be in service to the greater part.

Our human hands came here to work
To know the glory of sacrifice,
For those who come only to receive
Will find no light in the deepest night.

By silence did our toil endure,
A full oasis joined at the core,
Placing our faith in worlds beyond
That connect us to our Evermore.

Not by word of mouth or other sign
Did people gather by the base of the Light,
To open their hearts to the hum of the stone,
A peaceful retreat in the dead of night.

Now the rhythm beats to a different drum
And time calls us to follow her care,
The people are here upon her hour
To see the Light so bright and fair.

Now everything was finally set
With people, place, and time just right,
For the architect to pull the switch
And give the world its greatest light.

And the star did shine far and wide
Touching those upon distant shores
For when you turn on a light in the dark
The greatest wonders are for evermore

Yes, when you shine a light in the dark
The greatest wonders are for evermore,
Oh, the greatest of wonders
Are for ev-er-mo-re...

And love is the light we bring to the world
And love we must alight in each human heart,
For my love is with me now and I with her –
This is the seed of the Song of Songs.

Beautiful Traitor Books was founded in 2012 as an independent print-on-demand imprint to provide unusual and inspiring books for the discerning reader.

Our books are works that delve into various domains whether it is books for children, science fiction, social affairs, philosophy, theatre plays, or poetry. All the books we publish seek to explore innovative and creative ideas. Many of them also tell a good story - stories that have different perspectives on life and on the human condition. Beautiful Traitor Books is not only about offering the reader entertainment. We also seek to offer something that is like a nutrition; something of value that the reader can take away from the book. Good books function on more than one level. Put simply, we thrive on books that have the capacity to shift the reader.

Come and join the conversation – find out more at:
www.beautifultraitorbooks.com